THE SECRET OF
SPRING HOLLOW

THE SECRET OF SPRING HOLLOW

•

JAN WEEKS

AVALON BOOKS
THOMAS BOUREGY AND COMPANY, INC.
401 LAFAYETTE STREET
NEW YORK, NEW YORK 10003

PRINTED IN THE UNITED STATES OF AMERICA
ON ACID-FREE PAPER
BY HADDON CRAFTSMEN, BLOOMSBURG, PENNSYLVANIA

This book is dedicated to the memory of my mother,
Jean Fiser, and to Larry and Junie, who always knew I could.

Chapter One

A raw February wind raveled the dark clouds, sending them spinning and twisting across the peaks. Streamers of fog curled toward the small group gathered in the old family cemetery, and the mourners shivered in the damp chill. The twin wounds in the earth waited to receive the polished steel caskets.

Caitlin Morrisey pulled Linnie and Jeff closer, trying to shelter them from the pain of death as well as from the pervasive wind, but the cold was soul-deep. Reverend Dimmock's voice rose and fell eerily as the bitter breeze blew his words first to the mourners, then to the sur- rounding mountains. Linnie and Jeff stood straight and tearless, having cried themselves out in the days before the funeral. Caitlin blinked hard against the frigid wind; then her eyes filled with hot tears as she looked at the caskets. The tears chilled into icy rivulets on her face as the wind quartered around from the north to blow directly at her. She wiped them away, stiffening her resolve not to break down in front of her friends and neighbors. Lin- nie fumbled for Caitlin's hand, linking her gloved fingers tightly with her older sister's hand. Caitlin squeezed back. She was grateful for the touch. It seemed to ground her and lessen the unreality of the scene. Her breath caught in her throat, and her thoughts whirled in the same dance of death that had partnered them for the last few days.

Less than a week, she thought. Less than a week ago, their parents were alive and happy. Now they lay side by side in their caskets, still and cold and never coming back.

The mourners huddled together against the cold, their outlines blurred by the blowing snow, as the caskets were lowered into the frozen winter earth, neighbors and friends gathered in sorrow with the Morrisey children. The ropes slid smoothly through the pulleys; there were two muffled thuds as the caskets came to rest. The capricious winds stilled as Caitlin bent to scoop up a bit of dirt in each hand. The black earth was as cold as death, and she steeled herself to toss it into the waiting graves. A momentary stilling of the wind left the gathering enveloped by stark silence as she released the muddy earth, and then the wind whirled back, carrying her tiny moan to the sky and mountains.

Unable to think or move, she stared blankly at her muddy hands, the fingers splayed and rigid. Reverend Dimmock pressed a handkerchief against her cold flesh and patted her hand.

Moving slowly, as if trapped in a bad dream, Caitlin wiped the slick mud from her hands, then stepped back to stand with her brother and sister. She could feel Linnie's trembling as her sister's arms encircled her. Jeff stood stoic, swallowing hard, not blinking for fear his tears would destroy his composure. The neighbors closed in around them, silently escorting them from the graves. Caitlin stepped carefully, concentrating on avoiding the snow that had drifted along the path. At the gate of the cemetery, their friends and neighbors murmured condolences, and the soft words mingled with the wind to sound a dirge.

"So sorry . . . we called as soon as we heard . . . anything we can do . . . call us anytime . . ." The words swirled aimlessly around Caitlin and Linnie and Jeff, and they nodded and murmured, as if they were truly hearing what was said. The wind increased, lifting coat hems and plastering hair against faces. The mourners hurried away toward their cars and pickup trucks.

The three Morriseys squeezed into the cab of their pickup, and Caitlin rubbed her numbed hands together to warm them. She fumbled the key into the ignition, and the blue Ford fell into the line of vehicles leaving the cemetery. They rode in silence, each lost in memories and mourning.

Hard balls of sleet rattled against the windshield as a squall moved across the dying afternoon, and for a moment, Caitlin drove in a whiteout, dependent on memory alone to keep them out of the ditch. The road reappeared, and she turned into the lane that led to the ranch yard.

Cars and trucks lined the corral fence like docile horses waiting to be fed. The windows of the old house glowed with a warm light, welcoming the mourners to the gathering.

Caitlin eased the pickup into the parking space that had been left for them near the yard gate and turned off the ignition. They sat for a moment, listening to the *tick-tick* of the engine cooling. Then, reluctantly, Jeff opened his door, slid out, and offered a hand to Linnie. Caitlin drew a deep breath and let it out slowly, then pulled her coat collar tighter against the wind as she got out of the truck and hurried into the house after them.

She paused in the warm kitchen, alone for the moment, and listened to the low hum of conversation that drifted down the hall from the living room. Linnie and Jeff had already joined the crowd, and Caitlin followed, her steps heavy and slow on the polished oak floor.

"Cait, dear, come and sit down." Mae Bricklin, the children's godmother, took Caitlin's coat. Caitlin smiled at the older woman, grateful for her support. Mae's wiry, gray-brown hair struggled to escape from its bun at the back of her neck, and she pushed absently at it. Her face, still unlined after almost sixty years, creased with concern as she eyed her goddaughter.

"How are you holding up?" she asked.

"I'm fine," Caitlin replied. "Really. I'm okay." Her voice was normally low and slightly husky, but the strain and tears of the afternoon added even more huskiness. She cleared her throat and smiled at Mae.

Mae shook her head as if she found Caitlin's reply unconvincing, but Caitlin patted her arm and then moved around the edge of the crowded living room and sank into her mother's favorite armchair. She saw Linnie and Jeff already surrounded by some of their high school friends, and she was grateful to the students for their support. Linnie's lips were turned slightly up at something her best friend, Suzanne, had said; not quite a smile, but better than the frozen expression she'd worn since early morning. Linnie brushed her long blond hair back over her shoulders, and Caitlin saw her visibly relax. Jeff's dark head nodded in response to a comment from Todd, his best friend. Caitlin felt the atmosphere subtly change from one of deep mourning to one of sadness lightened by friendship. The finality of the service had served to release them all from the trancelike state they'd existed in ever since the accident. The sooner they could get back to normal, the better off they'd be.

"Cait, how're you doing?" Caitlin jumped as Tony

Black settled onto the arm of her chair and laid his arm across her shoulders. She hadn't seen him approach. She stiffened under his touch and shrugged slightly, annoyed by the intimacy. Tony owned a ranch not far from theirs, and the two families had been close when Tony's parents had still been on the home place. Now that they'd retired, moved to Arizona, and left the running of the operation to Tony, the elder Morriseys had gradually withdrawn from the friendship. Caitlin had never been fond of Tony. Ever since they'd been in junior high school, he'd tried to push himself into the position of boyfriend, but she'd managed to turn away his advances without alienating him.

"I'm fine," she replied, "but it's been a long day."

"You have been so brave, darlin'." Tony spoke softly and bent closer to whisper to her. His breath gusted across her cheek, and Caitlin flinched under its warmth. His grip on her shoulder tightened as he tried to pull her closer. "I notice Devlin didn't have the nerve to show up at the funeral," he continued. "It's probably a good thing."

"I don't want to discuss Connor Devlin," Caitlin said sharply. Her slender body tensed. "Excuse me, Tony. I have to circulate." She stood and smoothed the black dress over her hips. She smiled faintly to apologize for her abrupt departure.

Tony's lips thinned and his jaw hardened as he watched Caitlin drift through the crowd toward the buffet her friends had set up. She spoke and smiled and accepted condolences gracefully, the perfect lady, the perfect hostess. He pulled a pack of cigarettes out of his jacket and tapped one against his thumbnail, then shoved it back into the pack. He, too, began to circulate through the crowded room, stopping for a bit of conversation here and there, but edging closer to Caitlin all the time.

Ed Bauer, one of the Morriseys' oldest friends and the owner of a ranch several miles away, put his arm around Caitlin. His weathered, worn face was kind, and Caitlin had to choke back her tears at his words. "Cait, I'm so sorry," he said. "Your folks were the best. That accident was just pure bad luck."

"I know," she replied, attempting to smile. Her lips quivered, and she fought the tears that sprang so readily to her eyes.

He patted her back and gave her a little hug. "Now don't you go worryin' about anything. Me and some of the others've been feedin' your cattle and we'll keep right on doin' it. Are you goin' back to Denver?"

"I don't know yet," she said. "I'm so close to finishing the quarter, but I don't see how I can leave Jeff and Linnie here alone."

"Well, everything'll work out," he said, trying to comfort her.

The telephone rang. Mae answered, then held the receiver against her ample bosom as she stood on tiptoe and motioned to Caitlin. The girl excused herself from Ed and slipped through the crowd to take the call. She slipped around the corner into the hallway, holding a finger against her free ear.

"Cait, this is Jerrold Hirsch."

"Oh, hi, Mr. Hirsch." Caitlin puzzled over why the family attorney was calling.

"I'm sorry to have missed the funeral, but I was out of town on business and just got in. I need to talk to you. Soon. Can you come by the office first thing in the morning?"

Caitlin answered, "Sure, but didn't we cover most of the stuff the other day?"

"We did go over the will, but there are some other business matters that need your immediate attention." Tension quavered in his voice.

"What's wrong?" she asked.

"Cait, I'd rather discuss it in person. Tomorrow morning, please." He obviously wasn't going to go into any details right now.

"All right," she replied. "I'll be there at eight." Slowly she entered the living room and replaced the receiver, wondering what had happened. The will had been very clear and straightforward, leaving everything to her, to manage for herself, Linnie, and Jeff.

"What did Hirsch want?"

Caitlin spun around to face Tony. "Oh! Don't sneak up on me like that," she exclaimed.

"Sorry. You looked a little troubled. I thought I could help." Tony's hand on her shoulder irritated Caitlin, and she tensed, trying to keep from flinching.

"So what did Hirsch have to say?" he asked again.

Caitlin wanted to shout, "None of your business," but she stifled the words. Instead she said, "He wants to see me in the morning. And how did you know I was talking to Jerrold Hirsch?"

"I hope there's nothing wrong," Tony said, evading the question.

Caitlin wanted to slap him, and her right hand twitched as she clenched her fingers. She bit her lip and said, "I'm sure everything is in perfect order. Excuse me, please." This time she didn't smile to ease her rudeness.

As she mingled with the crowd again, she noticed Ed Bauer move to intercept Tony and engage him in a long-winded discussion of the price of cattle. She said a silent thank-you to Ed and vowed to bake him one of the peach pies he was so fond of.

The grandfather clock in the corner of the room boomed softly eight times. People donned coats and mufflers and picked up purses. Jeff, Linnie, and Caitlin thanked them for coming and accepted heartfelt hugs and sympathy. Tony lounged against the old, upright piano, trying to ignore Ed's lecture on the benefits of feeding hay versus silage. Caitlin could see from Tony's stance that he was prepared to outlast them all. She slipped through the diminishing crowd and whispered to Linnie and Jeff.

"Go up to your rooms right away."

"What's wrong?" Linnie asked.

"Tony looks like he's settled in for the night. If we go upstairs now, Mae can honestly tell him we've gone to bed. So come on, please?"

"Okay." Jeff and Linnie spoke together, a habit of theirs from childhood. As they said good-bye to their friends, Caitlin caught Mae by the buffet and explained the dilemma to her.

"Sure," Mae said, "you go on up. I'll take care of Tony." Her voice boded no good for him if he tried to linger. Caitlin stifled a giggle as she visualized Mae literally throwing Tony off the property. He wouldn't touch down until Sunday.

Jeff and Linnie had already gone upstairs, and Caitlin edged toward the staircase that led to the upper story. Ed still had Tony corralled in conversation, and she quickly tiptoed up the polished oak stairs to her room.

Her brother and sister were waiting, perched on the edge of Caitlin's bed.

"How weird!" Linnie exclaimed. "Having to sneak

out of our own living room. How come you wanted to get away from him so fast?''

Caitlin flopped beside them on the bed and sighed. "I don't really know. He's just been hanging around too much lately. And he was eavesdropping on a conversation I was having with Mr. Hirsch. He tried twice to find out what we talked about. I don't like him, and I don't like the way he's been poking into our business since Mom and Dad . . .'' Her voice trailed away, and they all sat silently for a moment.

"Yeah," Jeff finally said. "I've noticed how he's been hanging around, even before the wreck."

His voice trembled and broke on the last word, but he fought back the tears.

"I just can't figure out what he wants," Caitlin said as she smacked the mattress with her clenched fist. "I've never given him any reason to think that I care about him, but he's bound and determined that he's going to be more than a friend."

A soft tap sounded on the door. Caitlin jumped up, her hands against her heart. "Who is it?" she asked, fearing the worst.

"Just me."

"Oh, come in, Mae." Caitlin quickly opened the door, and her godmother entered.

"He finally left," Mae said, "but Ed practically had to drag him out. I told him you'd already gone to bed, and he was rarin' to come up here and comfort you. Can you believe the gall of that man?" She stood with arms akimbo, disgusted with Tony's lack of good sense and good manners.

"You're kidding," Linnie said. "He was actually going to come up to Cait's bedroom? What a jerk!" She flopped back onto the bed and groaned.

"That's for sure," Jeff agreed.

Caitlin rubbed her forehead with both hands. "That would be all I need. I'd probably have to bash him with a chair or something to get rid of him. He can't take a hint. Or," she said as she grabbed a wooden hairbrush from the dresser, "I'd have to turn him over my knee and give him a good hiding!" Her voice was an excellent imitation of one of their mother's threats, which she'd never carried out.

Mae's lips twitched, and Linnie and Jeff started to giggle. The thought of their petite sister turning Tony over her knee was too much for them. Caitlin joined in, enjoying the first laugh any of them had had since receiving news of their parents' accident. It was pure silliness, but as an antidote to fear and pain, it was perfect.

"Oh, boy!" Jeff gasped. "I can just see that. He'd never show up here again. And can you imagine what people would say if word got around?"

Caitlin collapsed on the bed, holding her sides. "Good night, you two. I can't take any more of this."

Linnie and Jeff held on to each other as they let the last of the laughter escape. Their mirth dwindled to a few hiccuping giggles. Linnie started the old childhood routine.

" 'Night-night," she said.

"Sleep tight," Caitlin replied.

"Don't let the bedbugs bite," Jeff finished.

"Come on, you two," Mae said as she ushered them to the door. "Morning comes early, and there'll be chores to do. Too many late nights take the starch right out of you."

Caitlin smiled as Mae closed the door. She heard Jeff and Linnie's footsteps in the hall and Mae's heavier tread on the stairs. Last muffled good-nights reached her before their doors closed.

They're such good kids, she thought as she flicked on the table lamp beside her bed and switched off the overhead light. The room glowed in the soft light cast by the rose-shaded lamp, and Caitlin felt an aura of comfort and, if not happiness, at least contentment filling her. She hung her black dress carefully back in the closet and shrugged into a warm flannel nightgown. February was cold in the Colorado high country, and she'd learned long ago that filmy nightwear was better left for tropical vacations.

She slipped between the sheets and curled up in a ball, waiting for her body heat to warm the bed. Slowly she stretched out under the two blankets and the handmade quilt. How comforting it was to be home, even in such tragic circumstances. She'd missed the quiet of the ranch and the childhood memories while she was away at college in Denver.

She reached for the light switch, and the room plunged into darkness. In less than a minute, Caitlin was asleep.

Chapter Two

"Caitlin, sit down. I'm afraid I have some very bad news." Jerrold Hirsch pulled the heavy, old-fashioned chair back from the desk and gestured for her to sit. The lawyer's face was creased with worry, and his movements were jerky. He was not the usually suave man of business she was used to dealing with.

Caitlin settled on the edge of the chair. She'd never seen him so upset, and it made her scalp prickle.

He sank onto the chair behind the desk, the sunlight streaming through the sheer curtains turning his curly gray hair into a white halo. He swiveled sideways, avoiding her eyes.

Caitlin's heart pounded, and she couldn't catch her breath. She felt as if she'd just run a mile instead of climbing one flight of stairs to his office. Her fingers tightened convulsively on her purse. His voice was rough and unsteady as he spoke.

"Cait, there's no money."

Stunned, she whispered, "None at all? What about their life insurance? What happened to that?" Her voice rose, and she clamped her lips together to get control. Not in her worst dreams had she imagined this.

Jerrold Hirsch swiveled back to face her. "Estate taxes took it all. When the government got through with those policies, there was barely enough to bury your parents."

The room swung around crazily, and she folded forward as her breath surged out in one explosive gasp. She felt as if she'd fallen from the hayloft flat onto the barn floor. Jerrold's grip on her shoulders kept her from falling off the chair. She vaguely wondered how he'd gotten around the desk so quickly. He eased her back and chafed her hands.

"Oh, Cait. I'm so sorry to have to tell you this. If only your father had made some provision . . . but it's pointless to speculate. Neither of them expected to die so soon. I'm sure they planned on turning everything over to you, or Jeff when he was older, just to avoid such a catastrophe."

Caitlin straightened and whispered, "What will we do? Where will we go? I know the ranch isn't paid for, and we still owe on the trucks." She extended her hands and looked at them helplessly, as if the answers lay in her palms, and if she only tried hard enough, she could find them.

Jerrold took her cold hands in his warm ones. "I'm sorry I shocked you. It's not all bad," he said. "I should have started with the good news. The vehicles and the house are free and clear. Your folks carried credit life insurance on the loans. And remember, your mother inherited the house and twenty acres around it. It's paid for. The only mortgage left is on the other thousand acres, and that annual payment was made when your father sold last year's herd. You have a home. All you have to do is sell off the thousand acres. And, of course, your Forest Service grazing lease is worth something to another rancher."

"No!" Caitlin jumped to her feet. "I can't sell the ranch. It's our home. I can't sell our home." Her voice broke and she covered her face with her hands. Her dark chestnut curls fell over her fingers as she rocked back and forth in the big chair.

"Be reasonable, Cait! The payment is over ten thousand dollars a year, due again at the end of November. How will you manage to make the payment?" Jerrold asked.

"I don't know," Caitlin replied. She stood and leaned against the stately mahogany desk for support. Her dark eyes had the look of a wounded deer, but she raised her head defiantly, and her voice was steady as she said, "But I'll find some way. That ranch is our home! We can't just give it up."

The lawyer touched her shoulder. His voice was conciliatory. "Well, you have several months to decide. Don't feel that you have to rush into anything. Let some time pass. Get some perspective. Incidentally, have you decided how you're going to manage the cattle you have now?"

Caitlin shook her head. "I don't know. Dad took care of all that. A couple of the neighbors have been feeding for us since the accident, but I can't expect them to continue to do it, and Jeff can't do all the chores. He's having a tough enough time in school as it is." She sighed. "I don't know what to do. Calving season's coming up, and we can't afford to hire help."

"Perhaps you could sell the herd," he suggested.

"Who'd buy at this time of year?" she asked. "Everyone I know has his own herd to take care of and doesn't need more cows, especially in the middle of the winter."

"Well, I'll ask around, if you'd like me to," he said. "If you could sell the herd, you'd have a little money to tide you over until you can get things under control."

Caitlin nodded. "Thanks. I guess that's the sensible

thing to do. Now I'd better get back to the ranch and see if I can get organized.''

He held her elbow as he guided her to the office door and held it open for her.

''Thanks, Mr. Hirsch. Sorry I fell apart,'' Caitlin said as she shifted her purse to shake his hand. ''I'll talk this over with Linnie and Jeff. We'll find a way, somehow.'' She raised her chin and managed a trembling smile before she turned away.

The door closed quietly behind her, and Jerrold Hirsch coughed and brushed the moisture from his eyes. It must be allergies, he thought. He hadn't cried for years.

Caitlin drove north out of town, lost in thought. The sun shone spring-warm from the February sky, and the black-top steamed as the snow melted. She scarcely noticed. The forty-mile drive back to the ranch was an endless journey, traveled by instinct alone. She was immune to the pristine whiteness of the huge valley that was walled with mountains shaded purple and blue under the pale blue winter sky. She braked hard as she realized that the pickup had passed the ranch entrance. She backed slowly and pointed the Ford into the lane, surprised to be home already. She remembered nothing of the drive from Montrose.

As she pulled into the yard, she looked at the house and outbuildings as though she'd never seen them before. The house was two stories, old but well kept. Her mother had been born here, and Caitlin had, too. In summer the huge old cottonwoods planted by her grandfather would cool the house, but now their leafless branches traced thin blue shadows across the snowy yard. The main barn and corrals stretched behind the house in a rough quarter-circle. The ''old barn,'' called that ever since she could remember, stood across the farmyard from the house. It had been used as a storage place for machinery ever since she was tiny. The building was still sound, in spite of its weather-beaten plank walls and rusty door hinges, and Caitlin had a fondness for it that had grown out of many hours spent in the hayloft looking for new kittens and outlaw hen nests.

Well, it was hers, free and clear. Hers and Linnie's and Jeff's. Her eyes burned as she thought of the scene in the attorney's office. She'd never give it up, no matter what she had to do to keep it.

She stepped carefully, picking her way through the morass of muddy slush the thaw had brought. She wiped her boots on the mat in the small, enclosed back porch, then went into the kitchen. The house lay silent in the afternoon sun. Caitlin had sent Jeff and Linnie back to school that morning, on the theory that normalcy could be restored only by doing ordinary things, and they wouldn't be home until at least four-fifteen.

She poured a glass of milk and took a leftover sandwich and a piece of pie to the round oak table, relaxing in the warmth of the sun as it poured through the big, south-facing windows over the sink.

Bless Mae's heart, she thought as she looked around the room. Her godmother had cleaned up after the wake. Then she'd slipped out and gone home while Caitlin slept. The white-tiled countertops gleamed against the yellow pine cabinets. The Mexican tiles on the floor had been swept, and the rag rugs that her mother had crocheted on winter evenings added patches of cheerful color to the room. She finished her snack and rinsed the dishes, leaving them to dry in the drainer on the counter.

She wandered through the silent house, straightening

a picture here, a doily there. She couldn't remember the last time she'd been alone in the old house. Maybe she never had. Her parents or Jeff or Linnie had always been somewhere around. Even when they'd been out working on the ranch or in the outbuildings, their presence still drifted through the rooms.

Now there was only empty stillness and too much tidiness. All the leftover pieces of their lives had been cleared away by well-meaning friends helping them cope and get ready for the funeral. Suddenly she couldn't stand the ordered, hushed room. She flung open the door and rummaged through the hall coat closet until she found her mother's knitting basket that had been tucked away. She placed it beside her mother's chair and made a resolve to practice the simple stitches her mother had taught her. She'd make the house live again. No more tiptoeing around the tidiness. She switched on the radio and found a classical music station. The low strains of Vivaldi's *Four Seasons* drifted through the house. She continued her tour, opening some sheet music on the piano's music rack, flipping open a magazine on the coffee table.

Finally she came to the room she'd been avoiding— her father's office. She opened the door. The room faced east, and the flat blue afternoon light reflecting off the shadowed snow made her uncomfortable. She fumbled for the drapery cords and pulled them almost shut, then snapped on the desk lamp, and a warm yellow circle illuminated the desktop.

She eased into her father's swivel desk chair. This had always been exclusively his room, and her invasion of it brought icy tingles to her skin. She'd never sat in this chair, and had only been in the room half a dozen times in her entire life. She looked at the tidy desktop. No good-hearted neighbors had straightened in here. Her father had always been fastidious in his habits, and the orderliness of the room was his doing. The only decorative touch was her parents' wedding picture, which sat on one corner of the desk. They smiled out at the camera, expecting the best, expecting to see their children grow and to spoil their grandchildren, not expecting to die. Caitlin choked back tears, determined not to give in to the grief that still tore at her heart.

Her hand shook as she pulled out the center desk drawer and looked at her father's almost fanatical tidiness. A leather-bound datebook lined up exactly with the checkbook. Pens and pencils lay neatly against a ruler. Small boxes of thumbtacks, paper clips, and stamps sat symmetrically in the shallow drawer.

She hesitated, then reached for the checkbook. She stifled the urge to look over her shoulder for her father's ghost as she paged through to the last entry. It was silly to feel so guilty about doing what needed to be done. The balance showing was nine hundred sixty-three dollars and thirty-nine cents. So there was a little money. Not enough to run the ranch for the next nine months, but there must be some way to raise the money before the next land payment was due. It was up to her to find a way.

She extracted the appointment book and leafed through it idly. Most entries referred to the usual things—dinner at the Gaylords', the church social back in January. She wondered where last year's book was. Dad never threw anything away. She investigated the two deep drawers on the right side of the desk but found only business receipts and bank statements, along with ranch records.

She walked to the bookcases that lined two walls of the room and ran her fingers along the spines. A light layer of dust clung to her fingers, and she made a mental note to clean the shelves. Animal husbandry and agricultural volumes predominated, but an occasional novel had sneaked in, and she smiled as she came across a well-used copy of *Wind in the Willows*. On the bottom shelf, she found what she was looking for: at least ten day-books, all identically bound and dated in gold on the spines. She crouched to pull out the one for the previous year.

The back door slammed, and Jeff's voice cut through the stillness.

"Cait! You home?"

"I'm in here," she called as she laid the datebook on the desk. She turned off the light and hurried toward the kitchen.

"So how was school?" she asked.

"Okay." Linnie shrugged. "A lot of kids avoided us, like they didn't want to get too close to us." She threw her books on the table and slammed open the cupboard door for a glass. The water gushed into the sink as she filled it, and Caitlin winced as her sister spitefully twisted the handle to shut the flow off.

"Yeah," Jeff broke in, "it was like we had a disease or something. I'm glad Todd stuck by me." His expression was angry and hurt.

Their pain hurt Caitlin. "That's a shame," she said, "but most of them haven't had parents die. They don't know how to deal with someone else's sorrow."

Linnie snapped, "How hard is it to say, 'I'm sorry'? At least then we'd have known they cared." Tears shone in her eyes, and she blinked rapidly.

Caitlin felt her sister's shoulders tremble as she hugged her close. "They do care, honey," she said softly. "They just don't know how to tell you, so they keep quiet."

"Well, it was weird." Linnie sniffed as she pulled away from her sister and opened the refrigerator.

"Don't eat too much," Caitlin cautioned. "You'll ruin your appetites. What do you guys want for supper?"

Jeff joined Linnie at the refrigerator and searched through its crowded contents. "Why cook, Cait? There's tons of food left. Why can't we just snack?" He bit into a cold chicken breast.

"Yeah. We've got to eat all this or it'll go to waste." Linnie added her argument to Jeff's.

Caitlin surrendered without a fight. "Okay, okay. Anything left over is fair game. Help yourselves." She brought plates and silverware to the table while the younger Morriseys loaded the old oak table with chips, chicken, cold salads, breads, and a carton of milk.

The sun dipped behind the mountains, leaving a clear, green sky in the west. The evening star hung over the tallest peak, bright in the gathering dusk. Caitlin loved to sit in the comforting warmth of the kitchen while the world outside sank into cold stillness. She tuned out the chatter of the two and felt peace stealing over her, as deep as the sky. This was still home, even though circumstances had changed, and it would be home forever, no matter what the future brought. The scraping of Jeff's chair brought her back to the present.

"I'd better get the chores done," he said as he stacked his plate and glass on the counter near the sink. "Rough and Ready are probably wondering where I am." He grabbed his coat from the peg on the porch and headed out to the barn to feed the horses and the chickens. Linnie ran steaming water into the sink while Caitlin scraped and stacked the dishes. Linnie hummed a current rock song while she washed the dishes, and Caitlin was relieved that her mood had lifted.

Soon Jeff clattered back into the entryway and pulled off his overshoes. "Whoo! It's gonna get cold tonight," he said as he slammed the kitchen door and hung up his coat. "Clear sky and already down to eighteen degrees."

"Did you happen to check the propane tank?" Caitlin asked.

"Yesterday we were still about half-full," he replied.

"Good. With a little luck, that'll get us through most of the cold weather." She pulled out a chair and seated herself at the table. "Now sit down, guys. We need to talk."

Her serious tone drew curious, half-frightened glances from the two as they arranged themselves around the kitchen table. They waited quietly while Caitlin marshaled her thoughts.

"First, we're broke." She paused, letting the shock sink in. She'd tried all day to think of a gentle way to break the news, but when the time came, she still hadn't thought of any better way than to blurt out the truth.

Jeff and Linnie looked at her, then at each other. Linnie traced a design on the tabletop with her finger. Jeff cleared his throat.

"What exactly do you mean by 'broke'?" he asked.

"I mean we have less than a thousand dollars. You know I talked to Mr. Hirsch today. It seems estate taxes took all the insurance money. All we have are the house and twenty acres that belonged to Mom." There was a sharp edge to her voice that brought their eyes to hers.

"You mean we don't own the rest of the ranch?" Jeff's face paled with shock.

Caitlin rubbed her temples to ease the niggling little pain that had crouched there ever since her conversation with the family lawyer. "No, but the annual payment's not due until next November, so we have a little breathing space,'' she added.

The kitchen was warm and cheerful, an oasis in the winter night, but the three felt as if a dark wind had slipped into the room and enveloped them in its frozen breath.

Jeff muttered something.

''What?'' Linnie asked.

''Oh, nothing,'' he said, tipping his chair back and crossing one booted foot over his knee. ''Just that this would be a good time for that old Spanish treasure to show up.''

''Oh, come on, Jeff,'' Caitlin scoffed. ''You know that's just a legend. The mountains are supposed to be full of buried treasure. Why, if all the stories were true, we'd be plowing up doubloons in the north pasture.'' She frowned, annoyed by his irrelevant remark.

Jeff scowled at his sister. ''All right, but legends start somewhere. There *could* be gold around here, and if we found it, we wouldn't have to worry, right?''

''It's a nice dream, but I'm afraid the only way we're going to save the ranch is through hard work and econ-omizing,'' Caitlin said. ''Miracles don't happen any-more.'' She pleated a napkin and smoothed down the crease before continuing. ''I'll call the university tomor-row and drop out. Too bad I couldn't go back for one more week. Then the quarter would be over.''

''Don't quit!'' Linnie and Jeff shouted together. Jeff sprang up and then had to grab his chair to keep it from crashing into the wall. ''You've got to finish.'' His voice broke, and he cleared his throat as he settled back into his chair.

Linnie went on, "We can stay in town with Mae. It's only for a week. I can drive the Ford, and Jeff and I can come out after school to do the chores."

"Sure," Jeff agreed. "Only a week? It'd be a crime to drop out now and lose a whole quarter's worth of credits. Besides, Ed told me last night he and some of the others will keep feeding the cattle as long as we need them to help."

"I know," she said. "He told me the same thing. But I'm still worried about the herd. We can't expect Ed to come running every time we need something, and calving time's coming up."

"We can handle it," Jeff said.

"No, we can't," his sister replied. "Dad could, but you two have school, and you can't be up all night for weeks on end. I can't, either. One person just can't do the whole thing."

She buried her face in her hands. Linnie reached to touch her shoulder.

"Don't borrow trouble," the younger girl said. "We can manage anything for a week. You go back to school, finish up, and then we'll find some way to keep going."

Caitlin looked at her siblings through unshed tears. They had all grown up fast in the week since the accident. Linnie sounded so much like their mother, always looking on the bright side, taking life one step at a time.

"Thanks, kids," she said as she pushed away from the table and stood up. "Let's sleep on it. Maybe things will seem clearer in the morning."

After washing her face and brushing her teeth, she tossed in bed, willing her brain to stop its mad dance of possibilities, but it seemed like hours before she fell asleep, and then she dreamed of caskets and classrooms, and hundred-dollar bills sprouting wings and flying south for the winter.

Chapter Three

"Now, Cait, don't argue." Mae Bricklin could steamroll over anyone, even on the phone. "Jeff and Linnie will come here, of course. I wouldn't think of letting you quit school with only a week left in the quarter."

"Mae, you must be a mind-reader," Caitlin said, laughing. "That's just what we were talking about last night. In fact, I was about to pick up the phone to call you when you called." She made shushing motions to Jeff and Linnie, who were dancing around the kitchen and laughing. "What? Sure, I have my return ticket."

"Good," Mae said. "There's a plane out of Montrose this afternoon. You can take Amtrak back. That way you can bring your things home. We'll pick you up next Friday."

"Gee, Mae, thanks for taking the kids, but I think I'll trade in my ticket and take the Chevy truck back to Denver. That way I can haul all my stuff, what little there is, and not have to worry about shipping it."

"Are you sure?" Mae asked.

"Really. It's the most logical choice." Caitlin didn't add, *And we need to save every cent we can.*

Jeff grabbed the phone from his sister. "Aunt Mae, you're a lifesaver. Hugs and kisses until this afternoon. Bye." He tossed the receiver and it caught on the phone,

25

effectively ending the conversation. He made a thumbs-up gesture. "Gosh, I'm good!"

"Too bad your talents are wasted on mere telephones," his younger sister scoffed.

Caitlin shushed them with a wave of her hand. "I guess you all have my life in order," she said, "and I'm glad you're my sister and brother." She enveloped them both in a bear hug. "Now get going. You'll be late for school." She pushed them toward the porch.

Jeff threw on his coat and ran to start the pickup while Linnie buttoned her parka and gathered her books together.

Caitlin heard the grinding of the engine; then it fired and settled into a comfortable rhythm. The truck door slammed and Jeff's footsteps pounded back toward the house. Another vehicle's engine sounded on the road and slowed as it made the turn into the lane. Caitlin idly wondered who was visiting this early in the day.

"Come on, Linnie. We gotta go." Jeff flung open the kitchen door, letting in a blast of cold air, just as a blue Blazer pulled up to the fence. He glanced over his shoulder at the car.

"Uh-oh, here's trouble," he said as he backed into the kitchen and closed the door, keeping one hand on the knob.

"Who is it?" Caitlin asked as she stood on tiptoe to look over his shoulder.

"It's Devlin," Jeff said.

His words chilled Caitlin like a November storm. "Oh, no," she whispered. A man bundled in a heavy sheepskin coat stepped out of the Blazer and started for the house.

Linnie grasped Caitlin's arm and clung to it tightly. Jeff stepped back to stand beside his sisters. He leaned forward, his hands bunched into fists, the classic fighter's stance. The porch floor creaked under the weight of their visitor.

Caitlin turned the doorknob and opened the door just as he raised his hand to knock.

"What do you want?" Her words grated harshly in the sudden silence.

He stepped back and scowled at her. "I came to talk business," he said. "May I come in?"

"We don't have any business with you, Mr. Devlin," Caitlin snapped. She tried to slam the door, but his booted foot slid out and kept it from closing.

"Get out!" Caitlin screamed. Jeff lunged forward, ready to fight the much bigger man, but Caitlin threw out an arm to keep him back.

Connor Devlin made no move to enter the kitchen, but his foot stayed put, blocking her efforts to shut him out. "I came to talk to you, Miss Morrisey, and talk I will, either in there or out here. Now we can do it easy or hard." His granite eyes bored into her brown ones, and his craggy face was set in a determined expression.

"Go on! Get out!" Jeff shouted as he pushed past his sister. Devlin glanced at the boy, then turned his attention back to the dark-haired woman who openly displayed her contempt for him.

Caitlin put a hand on Jeff's arm. "I'll handle this," she said to her brother without taking her eyes off their neighboring rancher.

Scowling at Devlin, she muttered, "Out there." With a look, she warned Jeff and Linnie to stay put, then stepped onto the porch. The entryway was cold, and she clutched her sweater tighter as she looked up at the bulk of the man who almost filled the small room. "Well?" she snapped.

"First, I want to tell you how sorry I am about your

folks.'' His eyes held hers, and there was genuine sorrow in them.

Her lips curled into a contemptuous smile. ''Sure. You're sorry, I'm sorry, we're all sorry, but that doesn't change things, does it?'' she said bitterly. ''What do you want?''

He winced at her words, but immediately his face reverted to its impassive expression. ''I want to make you an offer for your ranch,'' he said.

''What?'' Caitlin couldn't believe her ears. She took a half step back from their neighbor.

''I want to buy your ranch,'' he repeated. ''I'll give you top dollar for it. You're going to need money, and I need the land.'' His tone was rational and businesslike, as if they were discussing an ordinary transaction.

Caitlin shook, not from cold now, but from rage. She stepped toward him, her face flushed. ''Mr. Devlin, the only thing I need is for you to get out of my house and off my property! If it weren't for you, I wouldn't be needing any money. I'd still have my father and mother.'' She pushed at his chest with her right hand. Tears spilled unheeded down her cheeks. ''If you'd kept your cattle fenced in, my parents would still be alive.'' He had started to back up under her assault, but now he stopped dead.

''Now wait a minute,'' he said. ''I didn't have anything to do with that accident!'' His face reddened under its tan, and his voice rose.

''Oh, sure!'' she scoffed. ''*You're* completely innocent. It was just *your* cow that broke through *your* rotten fence just as Mom and Dad came around that icy curve. *Your* cow that sent them skidding off that cliff. If you'd kept your fence posts repaired, that accident never would have happened.'' She tried to say more but choked on her anger. She raised a hand to strike him, then let it fall to her side. Tears streamed unheeded down her icy cheeks.

Connor Devlin stood silently, helpless before her grief. He ran a hand through his thick, black hair and said quietly, "That fence post wasn't rotten. I told the sheriff that. Someone loosened it and left it lying down. It was easy for that cow to get through. I'd checked that whole line a couple of days before and there was nothing wrong then."

"Well, Mr. Devlin, I just don't believe you." Caitlin spit out the words. "My parents are dead. I have to drop out of college. And somehow I have to meet the mortgage payments. And it's all your fault!" Her clenched fist battered his chest with each word. "There's no way I'll ever sell you a foot of this ranch. It's ours and we're going to keep it. Now get out. The kids are late for school." She whirled away from him and ran into the kitchen and slammed the door in his face.

Linnie and Jeff stood in the middle of the kitchen, their arms around each other. Jeff's blue eyes smoldered and the muscles around his jaw were tight. Linnie smeared her tears away with the palm of her hand. Caitlin wiped her own tears away with the dish towel hanging by the sink, then tossed the towel to Linnie as she sank into a chair and rested her head on the table. Jeff put his arm around her shoulders. "It's okay, Cait. He's gone now," he said awkwardly. He had never known his grown-up sister to lose her self-control so quickly and so completely.

The Blazer's engine roared, and Connor Devlin drove out of their lives. Tension drained out of the room as the sound of his exhaust faded.

Caitlin straightened and took a deep breath to calm

herself. ''I'm all right,'' she said as she glanced at the clock. ''Look, you guys are late enough as it is. Get to school. But Linnie, be careful when you come out for chores tonight. There's another storm coming in.''

''Do you think you'll be able to leave for Denver?'' Jeff asked.

''I don't see why not,'' she said. ''The storm's not supposed to move in until later. I'll leave right away and run ahead of it. We'll just have to hope I don't get snowed in somewhere.'' Caitlin smiled to reassure them. She jumped up and hugged them both hard. ''Now go, go, go! You're late.'' She handed them their schoolbooks and shooed them onto the porch.

''Bye. See you next week. Don't worry about us.'' Linnie kissed her quickly, and then she and Jeff ran out to the idling truck.

Caitlin stood watching as her sister maneuvered deftly down the lane to the highway. It was a good thing that, as ranch kids, they'd all learned to drive early. Otherwise she wouldn't have been able to leave them here to take care of the farm while she finished her last week of college classes and tests.

She packed quickly, just her overnight bag with her cosmetics and a change of underwear. Most of her clothes were still in the apartment in Denver. She thought longingly of the two remaining quarters of college as she quickly washed and rinsed the breakfast dishes. If only there were some way she could manage to stay through the summer! Then she'd have her degree and be somewhat employable. She shrugged philosophically and rubbed lotion into her hands. Her first responsibility was to get Linnie and Jeff through high school. Maybe in a few years she could think about going back and finishing.

She moved through the house, checking window and

door locks, turning down the furnace and closing curtains against the cold, getting the house ready for a week of emptiness. Already the house felt lonely and colder. She shrugged into her parka, picked up her overnight case, and turned off the kitchen light. The lock snapped closed behind her as she left the house. She hurried to the truck and threw her overnight bag into the cab and climbed in. She scanned the sky as she pumped the gas pedal and turned the key. The earlier clear blue had faded to a high, white overcast, a sure sign of bad weather coming. Already the mountain peaks to the north were swathed in clouds. She backed the truck around, negotiated the frozen ruts in the lane, and pulled onto the highway. She picked up speed once she hit the blacktop, eager to cross Monarch Pass before the storm hit.

As she drove, she thought again of Connor Devlin, how his body had filled the porch, how his icy gray eyes had penetrated her soul. How could she ever forgive him for his carelessness? She never wanted to see him again. Ever. But her heart was troubled. His words had had the sound of truth. What if someone *had* tampered with the fence post? The idea of simple vandalism having such tragic consequences shocked her. *But then it doesn't really matter,* she thought savagely. *Mom and Dad are still dead, no matter how the fence got down. And it was his responsibility.*

She hardened her heart against Connor Devlin and drove toward Denver.

Chapter Four

The next week passed in a haze of packing and final exams. Her roommates sympathized and gave her a subdued going-away party. Her professors expressed the hope that she could come back soon to finish.

Friday afternoon finally arrived, and she checked the canvas tarpaulin that covered her belongings in the back of the truck. Her roommates were still in final tests, and Caitlin, feeling very lonely, pulled onto the freeway, driving away from a safe present toward an uncertain future.

The February storm had passed quickly, and an unseasonable warm spell had melted most of the snow. The roads were clear and dry as she drove west out of Denver and into the foothills. Once she left the metropolitan area, the road reverted to two lanes as it wound higher into the Rockies. She'd driven the route often enough to be sure of her way without having to consult a map.

She drove quickly and confidently, concentrating on how to earn enough money to keep the ranch going and the kids clothed and fed. Idea after idea raced through her head as she wound through the snow-covered mountains. Traffic increased as she approached the ski areas near Monarch Pass, weekend skiers making the most of what winter remained. As the truck started the long, winding climb up to the Continental Divide, the influx of vehicles dwindled, and Caitlin nudged the speed limit as she drove over the top of the pass and onto the western slope of the Rockies.

The late-winter sun sank behind the far peaks as she drove through Montrose, and the blue shadows of evening streaked the snowy hillsides. A cold, pink glow faded as the first stars sparkled like tiny, icy lights in the evening sky. She was only twenty miles from home. Jeff and Linnie were expecting her tonight, and she wondered if they were already at the ranch. The speedometer crept upward as she drove the last few miles.

As she turned into the lane, she could see light from the kitchen windows lying across the snow in pale yellow patterns. The door opened as she pulled up to the fence and parked. Jeff ran down the walk and caught her up in a bear hug. She hugged him back and ruffled his hair. "Hi, brat, where's your coat?"

"Ah, Cait, it's not that cold out," he protested.

"Cold enough to give you triple pneumonia," she replied. "Here. Take this suitcase in. We'll unload the rest of the stuff in the morning. I'm beat!"

"You look it," Jeff said as he caught sight of her face in the porch light.

Linnie met them at the steps and hugged her sister. "We're glad you're back," she said as they went into the kitchen. "Everything went fine. Mae spoiled us to death, but we're really glad to be home. It just wasn't the same, not being here." Neither Linnie nor Jeff had ever spent more than two nights in a row away from the ranch.

"I'm glad we're all home, too," Caitlin said as they crowded into the kitchen. "We're a family, and we belong together."

A pot roast simmered in the oven, along with potatoes,

onions, and carrots, and an apple pie rested on the counter. "You've been busy!" Caitlin exclaimed.

Linnie shrugged. "We figured you'd be tired, and pot roast isn't that hard to make." She opened the oven and stuck a fork in the carrots. She set the roasting pan on the stovetop and lifted the roast onto a platter, surrounding it with vegetables.

"That really looks good," Jeff said. "My stomach thinks my throat's cut, I'm so hungry." He snitched a carrot slice and popped it into his mouth, breathing with his mouth open to cool the food.

"We'll eat as soon as I make the gravy," Linnie said, stirring water and flour together and adding it to the pan drippings.

"I'll be down in a minute," Caitlin said as she hefted her suitcase. She went upstairs and washed quickly. The smells drifting up from the kitchen tantalized her as she hurried down the stairs and helped Jeff finish setting the table. Linnie set the steaming platter beside the bread and butter and the pie. They sat down and joined hands for grace. Two dark heads and one blond one bowed over the table.

"Thank you, Lord, for this food. Bless it and bless us who eat it. We are truly grateful for your bounty. Amen," Caitlin said.

"Amen," Jeff and Linnie echoed.

"So what happened while I was gone?" Caitlin asked as the platter passed from hand to hand and the clatter of silverware on china created a counterpoint to the conversation.

"Not much," Jeff said as he poured gravy over his vegetables. "Mr. Hirsch called and wants you to call him as soon as you can."

"I don't suppose he'll be in his office until Monday,"

Caitlin mused. "It couldn't be too urgent or he'd have called me in Denver."

"I think it was something about someone wanting to buy the ranch," Linnie said, buttering a slice of whole-wheat bread.

"Oh, no! Not Devlin again!" Caitlin groaned. "What do I have to do to get through to that man?" She rolled her eyes heavenward in exasperation.

"I don't think it was Devlin," Linnie said. "Mr. Hirsch didn't mention any names, but it sounded like the offer was made by a company or something."

"Well, I'm not going to worry about it now," Caitlin said as she ladled gravy onto her vegetables. "Monday's time enough to start worrying."

After the dishes were done and the kitchen cleaned, Caitlin called a conference. They sat around the table, sipping hot chocolate.

"You know we don't have a lot of money left," she said. The kids nodded solemnly.

"So what we have to do is come up with some way to make some. Let's brainstorm. I'll keep track of the ideas on this tablet." She tapped her pencil against the pad. "Then we can sort through them for the best one. Don't think, just say. We can always discard the really stupid ones later, but even stupid ones might give us an idea. Okay?"

"Sure," Jeff said. "We've done this in class."

"We could sell the ranch," Linnie said, making a face to show she was only kidding.

Caitlin wrote that down.

"We could become international jewel thieves," Jeff said.

"Oh, come on!" Linnie protested. "Keep it within the realm of possibility."

"No, that's okay," Caitlin said. "Any idea, no matter how dumb, gets written down."

Jeff stuck his tongue out at Linnie, and she sighed and looked away, pained by her younger brother's juvenile antics.

"We could get jobs in town," Jeff suggested, apparently trying to make up for the previous suggestion.

"Doing what?" Linnie wanted to know. "We're not exactly employable."

"Well, waiting tables or something," he said. "I could work at Tocko Tom's after school."

"But then who would do the chores? I'm not getting stuck with all the ranch work," Linnie said emphatically.

Caitlin wrote quickly. She encouraged them with a gesture. "Come on. Good suggestions so far. What else can you come up with?"

"We could rent out the spare room," Linnie said.

"Or we could live in the barn and rent out the whole house," Jeff said, laughing.

"I am not living in the barn!" Linnie shouted. "And that's final!" She sat back in her chair, arms crossed belligerently.

"Can't you take a joke?" Jeff said. "You sound just like a girl." His tone made it clear what he thought of girls, especially relatives.

Caitlin held up a hand to stop the bickering. "No, not in the barn," she said slowly, "but what's to keep us from renovating the old barn and renting out rooms to tourists?"

"What?" Jeff looked blank. Linnie leaned forward, frowning.

"Sure," Caitlin continued. "We could turn the old barn into a guesthouse and rent it to people who want to vacation in the West on a real ranch." She rubbed her eyes hard, trying to think. "I saw something like that in a magazine. There were these people who had a ranch and rented out their spare rooms to people who'd never been on a ranch before. Their guests could even help with the chores and stuff if they wanted to. They gave horseback lessons and did cookouts and all kinds of things."

"But wouldn't it take a lot of money to fix up the old barn?" Jeff asked.

"Let me think. The machinery can go to the new barn, or maybe we could sell it. We'll have to go through and see what we still need. I could see the bank about a loan. This could be the idea we've been looking for!" Her eyes sparkled as she looked at the others.

Jeff pushed back his chair. "Come on," he said as he shrugged into his denim jacket. "Let's go look."

The girls grabbed their coats, and the three plunged into the night, gasping as the cold air burned their lungs.

A three-quarter moon rode high in the sky, casting a silvery light over the mountains and valley. Their deep blue shadows raced ahead of them as they hurried across the barnyard. The rusted hinges of the old barn squeaked in protest as Jeff forced the door open. He fumbled in the darkness for the light switch.

The light from the one overhead bulb threw grotesque shadows across the floor, and the corners of the huge room lay shadowed and cold in the dim light. The three stood in the doorway surveying the mess. Years and years' worth of broken or unused machinery sprawled across the floor, jumbled together in a nightmare of twisted metal and wood. The loft sagged under its burden of old hay. The air smelled of ancient dust and long-gone animals.

"Maybe this wasn't such a good idea," Jeff said as he shivered in the night air that eddied from the open door.

Caitlin clambered over pieces of rust-flaked metal and weathered wood as she made her way deeper into the barn's interior. "No, wait. Don't write it off yet." She pointed upward. "The loft could be partitioned off to make a suite. Oh, not a luxury suite," she amended as her siblings grinned at each other, "but it could be at least two rooms. And we could have a couple more rooms put in under the loft. We could have this area"— her arm swept around to include all of the two-story barn space—"as a community kitchen and living room."

Linnie looked skeptical, but Jeff's face lit up. "Sure. We could have some big couches and a dart board. We could have a real neat place here." Already he and his sister shared the vision.

"But how are we going to pay for it?" Linnie asked.

"I'll go into town first thing Monday and see the loan officer at the bank," Caitlin said through chattering teeth. She pulled her coat closer around her as she made her way back to them and said, "Let's go back to the house. I'm freezing!"

Jeff shut off the light as the girls hurried across the frozen ranch yard, then sprinted to catch up.

Back in the kitchen, Caitlin poured more hot chocolate, and they settled around the table again. She passed out pencils and paper to the other two and said, "Let's list all the things we can do to make the barn habitable. Then we'll combine lists, and I'll have a plan to present to the banker."

The silence was broken only by the rough scratching of pencils for several minutes. Caitlin looked over the lists and chuckled. "I see we all think alike. 'Bathrooms' is number one on everyone's list. But there are some good ideas here, like having a supply of games and toys for children.'' Linnie smiled at Caitlin's praise.

''And a rope swing in the old cottonwood.'' That was Jeff's suggestion.

Caitlin folded her arms on the table and grinned at them. ''Guys, I think this could work.''

''Me too,'' Jeff said. ''It'd be kind of neat having different people around. I sure could lead trail rides.''

''Anything to get on a horse,'' Linnie teased.

''Well, sure,'' Jeff said, looking hurt. ''It's what I do best.''

Caitlin broke in. ''I'm sure that horses will play a very important part in our scheme, what with trail rides and maybe even some hayrides. We'll probably come up with a million more ideas before we're finished. Oh, gosh! Look at the time. You guys had better get to bed.''

''Ah, Cait, tomorrow's Saturday,'' Jeff complained.

''Yeah, but there's lots to do, and growing boys need their rest,'' she said in a caricature of a concerned mother.

He threw a wadded-up piece of paper at her and made a face. ''Oh, give it a rest,'' he said, but started for the stairs, Linnie right behind him.

Caitlin lingered in the kitchen to rinse the cups as the other two went up to bed. She switched off the light and stared into the moon-frosted night. Sadness and loneliness overwhelmed her for a moment as she thought of her parents and all the work that lay ahead if she and the kids were to make their plan work.

''Mama, Daddy,'' she whispered, ''help me do the right things. Don't let me lose the ranch.''

She wiped away tears as she climbed the dark stairs to bed.

Chapter Five

" "M_{r.} Faraday will see you now." Caitlin nodded
to the receptionist and approached the loan officer's desk.
All the words she'd carefully rehearsed jumbled together
in her mind, and she swallowed hard to moisten her
throat.

"Please have a seat, Miss Morrisey. What can I do for
you?" Mike Faraday indicated a chair and smiled at his
attractive applicant.

Caitlin sat down and clasped her purse tightly to control her shaking hands. "I'd like a loan, please."

The loan officer crossed his arms on the desk and
leaned toward her. "How much and what for?"

Caitlin's chin lifted and she met his eyes. "I need
about twenty thousand dollars so I can remodel our barn
and turn it into guest rooms."

He whistled softly. "What kind of collateral do you
have?"

Caitlin took the deed to the house and the twenty acres
out of her purse and handed it to Mr. Faraday. "I'll have
to hire an architect and construction crews, and have
some money left over for furnishing it," she said.

He rubbed his chin and cheek as he looked over the
deed. Caitlin chewed her lip and shifted in her chair,
waiting for him to speak.

Finally he laid the papers back on the desk and asked, "Do you have any experience running a resort?"

"Not really," she replied. "You see, our parents were killed recently, and I have to do something to meet the payments on the rest of the ranch and to keep my brother and sister clothed, fed, and in school. I really think this could work." Caitlin leaned forward, her brown eyes wide, her voice enthusiastic.

He saw the hope in her face, and he tried to soften the blow of refusal.

"I'd love to give you the money, but I need something a little more concrete," he said. "I could take your house and land as collateral, but I want to make sure you understand what you're getting into. I'd hate to see you lose what you have on a venture you aren't really prepared to go into. This is what I suggest." He tapped his finger lightly on the desk. "Draw me up a detailed plan with estimated costs, completion time, market research, and so forth. Then I might be able to help." He pushed her papers across the desk.

Caitlin fought back tears as she fumbled the documents back into her purse. This had seemed like the perfect solution to their problems a couple of days ago. Now it appeared that her great idea was just a pipe dream.

"Thank you," she managed to say as she stood and extended her hand. "I'll put something together and get back to you."

His hand clasped hers firmly. "Do that. I think you have a good idea, but it needs to be more concrete. Don't give up." His smile was sincere and encouraging, and Caitlin took heart.

"Thanks, Mr. Faraday." This time her smile was genuine and lit up her face like spring sun. She stepped jauntily toward the door, her faith in loan officers restored.

She squinted against the bright leap year sunshine as she climbed into the truck. The last day of February had brought a thaw, and the ground was slushy, but the air had a promise of springtime in it. Caitlin wondered whether March would come in like a lion or a lamb as she drove to Mr. Hirsch's office.

The lawyer greeted her warmly. ''Come in, Cait. I see you got my message.''

''Jeff said there was an offer for the ranch,'' she said as she took the chair he indicated.

''Yes, I've had quite a substantial offer—'' he began.

Caitlin interrupted. ''Not from Connor Devlin, I hope! I already told him I'm not interested in selling!'' She bolted out of her chair and paced the floor.

Jerrold's expression was puzzled. ''No, it wasn't from Mr. Devlin. It's from a corporation based in California. They've offered two thousand dollars an acre for the ranch. That includes the house and twenty acres that you own outright.''

''No way!'' Caitlin whirled to face him. ''That ranch is ours, and we're keeping it.'' Then she paused. ''At least we're going to try to keep it.'' She collapsed in the big leather chair and rubbed her forehead to ease the ache that had started behind her eyes.

''Why, Cait, what's the matter?'' His hand was warm on her chin as he turned her face to meet his eyes.

''Oh, Mr. Hirsch, I had a great idea of turning the old barn into a guesthouse and renting it out. But the banker turned me down. At least, I think he did.'' Briefly she explained what had transpired at the bank.

Then she added, ''He wants all this other information, and I don't have the money to pay an architect to come out and look it over. I need the loan just to get the preliminary work done!'' Her voice rose, and she slapped the desktop in frustration.

Jerrold Hirsch patted her shoulder. ''Calm down. I think there's a way to work it out,'' he said. ''I have a nephew who runs a construction company. If you have an idea of what you want, I could have him come out and give you an estimate of construction costs. He'd do it as a favor to me, since I've saved him a lot of time and trouble at various times.'' He chuckled. ''He owes me a big one, as he's always saying. Now's my chance to collect.''

''I couldn't ask you to do that,'' Caitlin exclaimed. ''That would be taking advantage.''

''Nonsense. It's just calling in a favor owed for a long time. I can't think of anything else I'd rather use it on. Maybe with concrete facts and figures, the bank will reconsider. And in the meantime, as long as you're in town, why not stop in at the library and gather some information about the rise in bed-and-breakfast establishments? If you can show Mr. Faraday that you have a market, he might be more easily persuaded to process the loan.''

Caitlin smiled gratefully. ''Thanks, Mr. Hirsch. You've given me hope again.'' She rose and shook his hand. ''I'll go to the library right away.''

''Do that,'' he said, ''and when this California firm calls back tomorrow, I'll tell them the offer was refused.''

''What corporation did you say it was?'' Caitlin asked as she buttoned her coat.

''I didn't say, but it's called Forrest-American. Apparently they do quite a bit of land speculation,'' he replied. ''It's funny, but Mr. Morgan didn't leave a number with my secretary. If he had, I'd call him today.''

''Well, he'll find out tomorrow,'' Caitlin said. ''By the

way, how did his company know that you're our lawyer?''

Mr. Hirsch stroked his chin absently. ''Now that, Cait, is a very good question. I'll have to find out when he calls back tomorrow.''

Caitlin paused, her hand on the doorknob. ''Please, if anyone else calls, turn down the offer. We're not selling. At least, not yet.''

''That brings me to the second piece of news,'' Hirsch said. ''There's someone who wants to buy your herd, and the offer is enough to give you money to live on for several months.''

''Who?'' she asked.

He shrugged. ''The offer was made through the stock sale broker in Montrose. I don't know who the ultimate buyer is, but I suggest you give the matter careful consideration. It could mean the difference between keeping the ranch or losing it.''

She bit her lip as she thought. This could be the answer to their immediate problems. They wouldn't have to rely on neighbors for help, and they'd have a little cash in hand. ''Go ahead,'' she said after a moment. ''I'm between a rock and a hard place, and I don't need to worry about a herd that's going to start calving in less than a month. And as you said, we need the money.''

He nodded. ''I'll take care of the details. I believe the cattle can be moved by the end of the week.''

''Fine. Now I'd better get to my research,'' she said. ''Mr. Faraday is going to take a lot of convincing.''

The old library was almost empty as Caitlin began her research. The quiet rooms and orderly shelves worked their familiar magic and soothed her. Problems couldn't exist in such an organized place.

Mrs. Fiser, the librarian, was extremely helpful, looking through the *Reader's Guide to Periodic Literature* and digging out the back issues of magazines that had printed anything about rural bed-and-breakfasts.

"I'm so excited for you," she said. "My niece and her husband spent some time on a ranch. They're from Los Angeles, you know, and they had the best time. As beautiful as your place is, you won't have a single empty room all year. Hunters and snowmobilers want a nice place to stay too, you know."

"Bless you, Mrs. Fiser," Caitlin said. "I'd forgotten all about them. I was planning just for the summer vacationers. Yes," she pondered, "about the only time we wouldn't be busy would be in the late spring, and that would be the perfect time for repairs and generally sprucing the place up."

"I know that you'll make a go of it," the older woman said as she handed over several magazines.

"Thanks for your confidence," Caitlin replied. "Now if I can just convince Mr. Faraday."

The librarian crossed her fingers for good luck and hurried off to help another reader, and Caitlin went to work sorting through the articles. After an hour, she'd found several on bed-and-breakfast places and small working ranches that catered to vacationers. Mrs. Fiser made photocopies of the stories for her and wished her luck again.

"I'll be sure to tell my niece and nephew about your place as soon as you get it open," she said. "They're due for another vacation, and they'd love to come to Colorado."

"Thanks again for all your help," Caitlin said. "If this doesn't convince the bank, nothing will." She tapped the stack of photocopied articles.

"Well, if you need anything else, just let me know. You don't even have to come in. Just call me," Mrs. Fiser said. "It sounds like a great idea. I wish you luck."

The warm sun had faded into a flat grayness when she came out of the library, and as she pulled into the farmyard, the first flakes of snow swirled gently from a sky gone dark and clouded. "Looks like March is a lion this year," she said to herself. The old barn stood faded and forlorn in the deepening dusk, and for a moment Caitlin doubted the feasibility of her plan. She stood shivering in the gathering dusk, wondering if she and her siblings could possibly succeed in creating a business out of an old barn and a few brand-new dreams. The phone rang faintly and she hurried into the house, dropping the pile of research on the kitchen table. She unbuttoned her coat as she reached for the receiver.

"Hello? Oh, hi, Mr. Hirsch."

"Hello, Cait. I just called to tell you that my nephew will be out Saturday morning to go over to the barn with you. If that's convenient, of course."

"Oh, thank you! So soon? I thought I'd have to wait for several weeks." Caitlin's excitement traveled down the wire, and the attorney chuckled.

"No, he just finished one big job and won't be starting another soon. All the other jobs are ones that his crews can finish on their own. So about two o'clock on Saturday?"

"That'll be fine. And thanks again for your help."

"I'm glad to help any way I can," he said. "Your parents would be so proud of the way you've handled this." He cleared his throat. "By the way, I spoke to a friend of mine in Los Angeles. He said he's never heard of Forrest-American, but he's looking into it. Directory Assistance has no listing under that name. Maybe tomorrow I can find out more when Mr. Morgan calls back.''

"How strange," Caitlin mused. "This whole thing has a bad feeling to it.''

"I agree," Hirsch said. "But don't borrow trouble. It should all be cleared up tomorrow. Let me know if there's anything else I can do.''

"I will. Good-bye." Caitlin hung up and clasped her hands as she fervently looked heavenward. "Thank you, thank you!" she exclaimed. Suddenly her world seemed very bright, in spite of the gloom outside.

She ran upstairs and changed into jeans and navy blue flannel shirt and boots. Throwing on her heavy work sweater, she skipped down to the new barn, stopping for a moment to try to catch the lazily floating snowflakes on her tongue.

The new barn's door slid open easily, and the dim interior smelled of hay and horses. Caitlin patted Rough and Ready, the two horses that worked the cattle in the summer and fall.

"Hi, you two," she said as she emptied buckets of grain into the mangers. Rough snorted as if to say, "About time. I was starving." Ready nuzzled close, waiting for her to scratch his muzzle and ears. "Yes, old fellow, you're a sweetheart," she crooned as she stroked the chestnut coat.

She brought buckets of water for each horse, and then ducked through the low doorway that led to the hen-house, a small room built into the corner of the barn. She checked the watering trough and picked up a bucket of grain. She eased through a second door into a fenced area that served as a chicken yard.

"Here, chick, chick, chick," she called as she tossed handfuls of cracked corn to the ground. The chickens flocked out, clucking and chuckling as they foraged for the kernels on the whitening ground.

Caitlin threw out a last handful and went back into the coop. Several nests contained brown eggs, and she enjoyed the smooth, warm feel of the fresh shells as she laid them in her egg basket. She set the basket inside the barn, fastened the inside door again, and went back out into the run to shoo the stragglers back into the coop. "It's going to be a blustery night. You don't want to be out in this," she said to one reluctant clucker.

The evening chores were done, and she closed the barn securely. The storm-dark evening wrapped her in a whispering cocoon of snow, and she moved quickly across the barnyard. Above the low moan of the wind, she recognized the sound of the Ford. The kids were home from school. The blaze of headlights caught Caitlin as Linnie swung into the parking space by the fence.

"Hey, Cait, did you do the chores already?" Jeff shouted. He'd noticed the egg basket right away.

"Sure did. You lucked out again," she called back.

"Gee, thanks," he replied as he jumped out of the truck. "With all the homework I've got, I can use the time." He made a big show of hefting his backpack to prove how much work he had.

"So how did it go at the bank?" Linnie asked as she skipped around the truck to the gate.

"Come on in and I'll tell you about it while I fix dinner," Caitlin said.

The smell of browning meat and onions filled the kitchen as Caitlin started the spaghetti sauce. Linnie rummaged in the refrigerator, looking for the salad ingredients. Jeff sliced French bread and spread it with butter, then sprinkled on garlic powder. Caitlin talked as she cooked.

"I can't believe he wouldn't give you the money," Linnie said after Caitlin had told her story.

"Well, I was pretty mad at the time," Caitlin admitted, "but after I calmed down, I realized we have to have more than just dreams on paper. In fact, I went to see Mr. Hirsch afterward, and he has a nephew in the construction business who's coming out Saturday afternoon to look at the barn and give us an estimate of what it'll take to get it in shape. I've got a ton of articles about successful businesses like this, and I don't see how Mr. Faraday can turn us down again, once he sees the figures. I found out a lot about what we should charge, too. You know, we didn't even think about that the other night. We'll start with a flat rate, then charge extra for more people. Do we want to include all meals in the price, or just breakfast?" She looked at the others.

Linnie stopped shredding lettuce to think about the question. Jeff shrugged. "I don't know. Whatever you want to do."

"I think that being so far from town, we've just about got to offer two meals a day. I don't want to mess with lunch, but breakfast could be simple—eggs, bacon, muffins. Then we could do barbecues or family-style meals at night. I'm sure that with a refrigerator and a stove, people could manage to fix their own lunches, if we provided the food," she said. "We'll include that information in the brochure."

"Brochure?" Linnie questioned.

"I checked with the printer. We can have some nice two-color brochures printed. They won't be slick and fancy, but I can do the lettering and artwork. We'll also have to advertise in some national magazines, and those ads will have to go in right away if we want any response for this summer."

"When do you think we can open?" Jeff asked. His blue eyes widened in excitement.

Caitlin stirred tomato paste and canned tomatoes into the browned meat as she answered, "I'd like to be open by the end of May, in time for summer vacations. But I can't really plan anything until I've talked to Mr. Hirsch's nephew and found out how long renovation will take."

Jeff reached for an apple, and Caitlin threatened him with the spaghetti spoon. "Not now. It's too close to supper."

"Come on," he complained. "The sauce has to simmer at least an hour."

"Well, okay," she conceded.

"So do you think we should get a satellite dish and a TV for the common room?" Jeff asked.

Caitlin shook her head. "I thought about that, but what we're offering is peace and quiet. Our guests will have to get along without television, just as we have all these years. I thought, though, that we could put in a wall of bookshelves and pick up some used books at the flea market. With games and books and fresh air, maybe they won't have time to get bored," she said.

Linnie used the knife to slide chopped tomatoes off the cutting board into the salad. She agreed with Caitlin. "Let's keep it rustic. Besides, have you seen what satellite dishes cost? Thousands of dollars!"

"There's that," Jeff agreed. "I guess we'll have to be thrifty if we want this to work, huh?"

"Yes," Caitlin said. "We're all going to have to put in a lot of hours and a lot of work to get this thing off the ground. You know that we don't have much money in the account, and even if we get the loan, we'll have to conserve our cash. Whatever we can do ourselves instead of hiring someone to do will give us that much more money for the land payment.''

''By the way, what did Mr. Hirsch want?'' Jeff asked.

Caitlin set a pot of water on the stove to boil. ''Some corporation from California wants to buy the whole place, including the house and the twenty acres Mom left us. Of course I told him no,'' she said in answer to their stricken looks. ''We're not giving up our home. I don't care what happens. We may lose the rest of the land, but we won't leave this house. I promise you that.'' She thrust the wooden spoon into the sauce and stirred vigorously, as if the dinner had suddenly spoken up and had disagreed with her.

''He had some good news, too,'' she continued. ''The stock sale broker has a buyer for the herd. That means we'll have a little money to get by on until we can get the guesthouse up and running. The herd may be gone by the end of the week. It's a good thing that Dad had brought them all into the nearest pasture. I sure couldn't drive them out of the timber by myself.''

''Whew!'' Jeff sighed. ''I was really worried about calving time. Ed and the others'll have their own herds to calve. They wouldn't have time for us.'' His relief was evident. Even though he was strong for his age, he and his sisters wouldn't have been able to cope alone.

''They've really been great,'' Caitlin said. ''I know it hasn't been easy for them to keep feeding them the last two weeks. We'll have to have a get-together to thank them.''

Linnie spoke as she chopped lettuce and other vegetables for a salad. ''Maybe our luck is turning. Maybe this is a good omen, and the bank will let us have the loan, and our business will be a success.''

Caitlin crossed her fingers and raised her eyes heavenward. ''I hope so. We need all the luck we can get. Is the salad done, Linnie?'' she asked.

''Yeah. All it needs is dressing.''

''Go ahead and have that while the spaghetti cooks,'' she said as Jeff eyed the apple dish again.

The talk at dinner revolved around plans for the barn.

''You've got some great ideas,'' Caitlin told the other two. ''I really think that this can happen if we all pull together.'' She paused, swallowing hard over the lump in her throat. ''I couldn't do this without your help.''

Jeff shrugged as he reached for another piece of bread. ''Heck, we're a family. We have to work together. Besides, it sounds like a lot of fun.''

''Well, there'll be a lot of work before the fun starts,'' Caitlin warned. ''Don't get upset if I nag you. When deadlines are involved, there's no time for wounded feelings.''

Dinner over, Caitlin said, ''You two get your homework done. I'll clean up in here.''

Linnie and Jeff went upstairs without protest. They both had tests in the morning and were happy to get out of kitchen chores.

Later, as Caitlin undressed for bed, Linnie tapped on her door.

''Can I come in?'' she asked, sticking her head around the door as Caitlin sashed her blue woolen robe tightly.

''Sure. What's on your mind?'' Caitlin smiled at her sister as she turned down the covers.

Linnie sat gingerly on the edge of the bed. She twisted the class ring on her right hand and chewed her lower lip. Caitlin knew something was bothering her but waited for her to speak.

''What if you can't get the loan? What if the whole

thing doesn't work? What will we do then?'' Linnie's face creased as a stray tear trickled down her cheek.

Caitlin sat down beside her and pulled her close, feeling much older than twenty-two. ''I'm not going to sell the house, if that's what you're worried about,'' she said. ''It's ours, free and clear, and it'll stay that way. There's no way we'll ever sell,'' she assured the girl.

''But what if—''

Caitlin put her fingers over Linnie's lips.

''No 'what ifs' allowed from now on,'' she said. ''We're going to make it. Don't borrow trouble.'' She chuckled softly. ''We'll probably have enough worries as it is without inventing new ones that may never happen.''

''Okay.'' Linnie wiped her cheek and stood up. She looked much younger than her seventeen years. ''I'll quit worrying and do my best to help.''

Caitlin gave her a quick hug. ''I'm counting on you,'' she said.

Chapter Six

Richard Jones didn't fit Caitlin's stereotyped image of a construction worker. He was fairly young, in his thirties, she guessed. Under the heavy coat his body was straight and slim, and his dark hair and eyes could have come right out of a television commercial.

"What exactly do you want done?" he asked as they tramped through the still-falling snow to the old barn. March was living up to its ferocious start.

"I was thinking of putting in some private rooms and a large common room with cooking facilities," Caitlin said. "Each room will have its own bathroom, of course, but I'm open to suggestions. I guess Mr. Hirsch explained my predicament to you." She glanced up at his classic profile.

"Yes, he did," Richard answered. "It's going to be tough, but you seem to want to make a go of it. How soon do you want to be operational?"

"Well, I'd like to be open by the middle or latter part of May to take advantage of the summer vacation season. That's a little over two months. Do you think we can be ready by then?"

"We'll see," he said dubiously as he opened the old barn door for her.

Caitlin switched on the light. The heaped machinery and ancient timbers looked even grimmer in the gray light that filtered through grimy windows than they had on the night the Morriseys had made their first foray into the barn. Richard moved slowly around the ground floor of the barn, sidestepping hay rakes and plow tongues. Caitlin waited anxiously for him to say something, anything. He stopped and craned his neck to look up at the hayloft, which filled half the barn. He pulled a small paperback notebook out of his jacket pocket, made some notes, and continued his tour. He crawled back under the loft, agilely climbing over the old machinery and tools piled there. Caitlin heard thumpings and bangings on the walls of the old building, and was just about to call to see if he needed help when he reappeared, dusty but intact.

His dark eyes sparkled and he grinned at her. "I think we can do it," he said, putting the notebook back in his pocket. "Convert the loft into a two-bedroom suite with a shared bath and build two self-contained rooms underneath, then use this open area for a common area. How's your water supply?"

Caitlin spent the next half hour answering questions about wells, septic systems, and other crucial matters. They paced around the old barnyard, and Richard made more notes.

"Okay. I think that's all. I'll have a crew out here by the end of next week, if you can get the loan and I can get the permits. Do you have an architect in mind?"

"Not really," Caitlin said. "I haven't had time to think that far ahead. But you do think we could be open by the middle of May?"

"I don't see why not," he replied as they walked back toward the house. "The construction will be simple enough. There's a guy I know just starting out as an architect. He's just out of school, but I've seen a few of his projects and I think he'll do a good job for you. Want me to send him out?''

''That would be wonderful!'' Caitlin exclaimed. ''I wondered how I would find someone. I was thinking of hanging the yellow pages on the wall and throwing a dart.''

His laugh rang in the frosted air, and he said, ''We can do better than that.''

He opened the door of his truck and Caitlin shook his hand. ''I can't thank you enough for helping me out like this. I never expected to get started so soon.''

''No problem,'' he said as he climbed into the cab. ''We're not swamped with work this time of year, and the crew will be glad to be working mostly indoors.''

Caitlin waved through the falling snow as he drove away, a strange fluttering in the pit of her stomach. It was possible. They were actually going to succeed with this plan that had serendipitously arrived at their kitchen table. She hugged herself in excitement, not feeling the chill of the wind, and ran back to the house.

Linnie and Jeff were waiting to ambush her as soon as she entered. ''What happened?'' Linnie grabbed her sister and shook her in mock anger. ''What did he say?''

''We can do it,'' Caitlin said.

''All right!'' Jeff punched the air and raised his hands in the fighter's classic sign for victory.

''He lined it out pretty much the way we did the other night,'' Caitlin said. ''And he even knows an architect that's just getting started, so we can begin right away, if I can get the loan.''

Jeff reached for his coat and said, ''Let's start moving junk out of there. Then we can see what goes where better.''

''Don't get too carried away,'' Caitlin cautioned. ''I

still have to convince Mr. Faraday. Remember? Besides, it's time for lunch.''

Jeff grinned. ''How can he turn us down? Didn't Mr. Jones say we could do it? What more does Mr. Faraday want?''

''It's hard to tell, but I'm sure he'll think of something,'' Caitlin said as she buttered slices of bread for sandwiches.

''Cheer up, Cait,'' Linnie said. ''It'll all work out. You'll see.'' The younger girl stacked lunch meat, cheese, and lettuce on the bread.

Their enthusiasm buoyed Caitlin, and she smiled at them. ''You sure are good for me. As long as we don't all get discouraged at the same time, we'll be fine.''

''Great idea!'' Jeff exclaimed as he popped the last potato chip into his mouth. ''I'll make up a depression schedule so we'll all know when we can and can't be depressed. That way we only allow one depression at a time, and two cheerfuls beat one depression.''

By midafternoon the snow had stopped, and a watery sun tried to fight its way through the flat grayness of the sky. Jeff wandered upstairs to do his homework, and Linnie took over the upstairs sewing room to finish a project for 4-H. Caitlin sat alone at the kitchen table, arranging and rearranging columns of figures, projections of profits, and estimated expenses, and wondering if any of it would persuade Mr. Faraday to give her a loan.

A car pulled into the ranch yard, and Caitlin pulled the curtain aside to see who had arrived. As always in ranching areas, the visitor came to the kitchen door, not the front door.

Caitlin recognized Tony's black car. ''Oh, great!'' she muttered. ''I wonder what he wants.'' She toyed with the idea of not answering the door, but both of the trucks were parked in plain sight, and Tony had already seen her. He waved and ran up the steps. Caitlin sighed and let him in.

"Cait, it's good to see you," Tony said and gave her a quick hug. Caitlin moved deftly out of the embrace and said, her voice cool, "Let me take your coat. What are you doing here?"

Tony smiled. "That's not a very warm welcome for such an old friend."

Caitlin shrugged. "Sorry, Tony. I'm not in a very good mood. I've been going over figures all afternoon and worrying about the bank."

Tony looked at the papers scattered all over the table and whistled softly. "You're working too hard. What is all this?" He shuffled through the papers, and Caitlin had to resist the urge to grab them and hide them. He had no business pawing through her things. Her palm itched to connect with his face, but she suppressed the urge.

"It's the newest venture of the Morrisey crew," she said, keeping her tone light. "We have to have some way to earn money to keep the ranch going, and this looks like the best way."

"Bed-and-breakfast?" Tony read from the sheet he held. "Dude ranch? Country vacations? What's going on?" He crossed his arms and leaned against the table, frowning at her. Caitlin knew she'd never get rid of him until she explained the project.

"We're going to convert the old barn into tourist rooms and offer two meals a day to people who want to vacation in the peace and quiet of the mountains."

"Oh, come on. You've got to be kidding." Tony's voice was sharp, and he paced the kitchen, scowling at her. "You don't know the first thing about running a business."

"But I can learn," she snapped, "and so far, no one's come up with a better idea." She crossed her arms and scowled back at him. If he wanted a stubborn contest, she vowed that he'd met his match.

Tony put his hands on her shoulders, ignoring the way she stiffened under his touch and turned her head away. "I have a better idea," he said. "I was going to wait for a while, seeing as how your folks just died and all, but if you're this desperate for money, I guess I'll take my chances with my proposal."

Caitlin pulled away and stared at him. "What are you talking about?" she whispered.

Tony smiled and held out a hand. His voice was low and sincere as he said, "Cait, I love you. You know that. I wanted to wait until you finished school to say anything, but circumstances have changed. Cait, will you marry me?"

Caitlin collapsed into the nearest chair. She leaned her elbows on the table and ran her fingers through her short curls, not looking at him.

"This . . . is too sudden," she murmured as tears welled in her eyes.

"Oh, Cait, don't cry." Tony knelt beside her and put his arms around her. "I should have waited, but I can't stand to see you so worried about money and keeping the ranch going. I can take care of you, and Jeff and Linnie, too. There's room at my place, or we could all live here. Please let me help you. Don't try to shoulder all your problems by yourself," he pleaded.

He handed her a clean handkerchief, and she wiped her eyes. "I'm sorry," she said. "Your proposal took me

by surprise, and when I thought about Mother and Dad
. . . I just fell apart.''

''I understand. I'm sorry I brought it up so abruptly.
But Cait, think about it. You could do a lot worse than
me, and you know I'll be good to you.''

He gazed deeply into her eyes. His sincerity stung her.
How could she hurt him? But she just couldn't bear the
thought of marrying him.

''I really can't talk about it right now,'' she said. She
pushed back her chair and went to the coatrack. ''Too
much has happened too quickly. Here's your coat. I think
you'd better go now.''

Tony shrugged into the heavy sheepskin coat and nodded. ''I understand. But don't think I'll give up.'' He
smiled tenderly at her. ''I do love you, and I'll wait however long it takes. If you can't think of me in a romantic
way, at least think of me as a good friend.''

''Thanks, Tony,'' she said, repressing a shudder. ''I
appreciate that.'' She opened the door. A few flakes of
snow swirled into the room on a blast of cold air. The
sun had lost the battle, and a new storm drifted in from
the west. Tony pressed her hand tenderly, but didn't try
to kiss her. She murmured good-bye and closed the door.

''Is he gone?''

Caitlin whirled around.

''Linnie!'' She gasped. ''You startled me. How long
have you been there?''

Linnie sidled into the kitchen. ''I heard almost everything,'' she said without regret. ''You're not going to
marry him, are you?'' She frowned and picked at a
cuticle.

''No way! We'll never be that hard up,'' Caitlin
answered.

''Good. If you loved him, I'd run away from home,''

Linnie said as she sat down at the table. Caitlin sat down, too, and covered Linnie's hands with hers.

"Looks like you get to stay, then," she said. "I don't love Tony, and I won't marry him under any circumstances."

Linnie said, "I don't know what it is about him, but I never have liked him, and I don't trust him. He reminds me of something that lives in a cave or under a rock."

Caitlin laughed at her sister's description of Tony, but had to agree. "There's something about him that makes my skin crawl. He's too . . . too secretive. Oh, I know he makes a big deal of being up front, and his little-boy honesty act has quite a few people fooled, but there's a lot about himself he's keeping hidden. He really makes me uncomfortable."

"Me too. And Mom and Dad never really liked him, either. After his dad turned the ranch over to him, you remember, when he and Tony's mom moved to Arizona, he really started to think he was somebody. He's been running the place down slowly ever since."

"Well, you don't have to worry about him," Caitlin said. "How's your dress coming?"

Linnie said, "That's the reason I overheard him proposing to you. I'm having trouble putting the sleeve in. Could you show me how to gather it?"

"Sure." The sisters spent the next half hour in the sewing room, working and talking happily. Tony was forgotten.

"Well, it looks like you've got sleeves mastered," Caitlin said as she stretched and yawned. "I think I'll take a walk and get some fresh air. I'm about to fall asleep."

Linnie looked at her curiously. "It's snowing and it's almost dark. Hadn't you better wait until tomorrow?"

Caitlin smiled at her motherly tone. "I need some exercise, and I won't go far. I'll be back before full dark. Would you start the potatoes for me? We're having them mashed to go with the pork chops."

"Sure," Linnie said as she folded up her sewing.

The phone rang, and Jeff yelled, "I've got it."

Caitlin and Linnie clattered down the stairs.

"It's for you," Jeff said, holding out the receiver to Caitlin. "It's Mr. Hirsch."

"Thanks. Mr. Hirsch?"

"Hello, Cait. I thought I'd let you know that I heard from Mr. Morgan at Forrest-American."

"Really?" Caitlin pressed the receiver closer to her ear. "What did he say when you turned him down?"

Hirsch hesitated. "He didn't say anything. He just hung up. I didn't even get a chance to ask for his phone number or business address."

"How strange!" she said.

"Strange indeed. I haven't been able to trace the company at all, and I have extensive contacts in L.A.," he said. "And I have to wonder why a nonexistent company would offer you cash for your ranch."

"Cash?" Her grip on the receiver tightened.

"Yes. As soon as I answered, he said to make sure you—he actually said 'the owner'—knew that the entire sum would be paid over at once when the deal was complete." He sighed gustily.

"Well, it doesn't really matter," she said. "I wouldn't sell out for cash, not for any amount of money, so I guess we'll just have to chalk it up as a weird experience."

"You're right, but it still bothers me," the lawyer said. "But I'm not going to lose sleep over it."

"Me neither," Caitlin replied. "Thanks for calling."

She hung up and stood still for a moment, her hand on the receiver.

"Well?" Linnie asked.

"Nothing. Mr. Hirsch just called to let me know he'd rejected the offer to buy the ranch. Now I'd better get my walk in before it gets too dark." She bundled into her parka and pulled on hand-knit woolen mittens and a matching stocking cap, gifts from her mother.

Fat snowflakes swirled in the dim twilight as Caitlin crossed the ranch yard and climbed over the corral fence. She set her face to the wind and trudged out across the pasture. Small drifts of snow made walking difficult, but she pushed forward, enjoying the work, the walk, and the cold March air. Too much sitting around made her nervous, and she'd been too wrapped up in her problems the last few days to get any exercise.

She paused and looked back. The lights from the house reflected on the falling snow, showering the deepening night with a veil of pale yellow. She thought she saw Linnie moving around, getting supper started.

Just a little farther, she thought, and plunged back into the strengthening wind. The snow thickened and all horizons vanished in the dusk. Caitlin had a feeling of being caught in a void, lost forever in a gray blankness. She shook her head angrily. "Knock it off," she admonished herself aloud. "You've walked this pasture a thousand times. You could find your way back blindfolded."

She stopped again. The lights from the house were almost obliterated by the storm, and she shivered. A sound caught her attention, a faint engine whine tossed on the wind. Off to the north, a tiny flash of light pierced the night, and the wind carried the sound of an engine struggling in low gear to her straining ears. She strained to see better and realized that there was no road in that direction. Someone was driving across their ranch!

Caitlin stared hard into the night, marking the location of the light in her memory. Whoever it was had to know he was trespassing. The only way onto the ranch to the north was through a gate secured by a chain and padlock. She hurried back through the thick snow, grateful now for the wind behind her, pushing her homeward.

Jeff and Linnie looked up as she burst into the kitchen.

''What's up?'' Jeff inquired. ''You forgot to brush the snow off.'' He pointed to the growing puddle on the floor.

''Don't worry about that,'' Caitlin said. ''There's someone driving up across the north pasture. I'm going to call the sheriff. Whoever it is is trespassing, and tearing up the pasture, to boot.''

''I could go out and take a look,'' Jeff offered.

''No,'' she said as she picked up the kitchen extension and dialed the sheriff's office. ''I don't want you running into any strangers. Any friend or neighbor would just come and ask for permission.'' She propped the receiver between her shoulder and ear as she pulled off her mittens and unbuttoned her coat. ''Oh, hello. This is Caitlin Morrisey. Someone's broken through one of my gates and is driving across my pasture. Can you send someone out to see what's going on?''

''It'll be a while,'' the dispatcher said. ''We had a five-car pileup east of town, and all available personnel are out there. Several people were hurt.''

''Oh.'' Caitlin thought a moment. ''Well, it's probably nothing, but if someone can come out, I'd really appreciate it.'' She gave their route and box number to the woman. ''At least make a note that I called, will you?''

''Certainly.'' The dispatcher sounded miffed. ''All

calls are logged in. I'll send someone out as soon as possible.'' The phone went dead and Caitlin hung up.

"I'm afraid I ruffled some feathers,'' she said ruefully. "The dispatcher thinks I was questioning her competence. But someone will be out when they get an accident cleared up.''

The storm worsened as the hours passed, and Caitlin gave up hope of seeing a lawman that night. Jeff and Linnie were already in bed, and she was fighting drowsiness when a sheriff's car pulled into the yard.

"Please come in,'' she said, holding the door open for the deputy. He carefully wiped his feet and shook the snow from his cowboy hat before he entered the kitchen.

"You reported a trespass?'' he asked. His gold name tag identified him as Deputy Schroeder.

Caitlin nodded. "Yes. There was a vehicle crossing our north pasture. No one has permission to be there, and there's nothing beyond there except our Forest Service lease land.''

"About what time was that?'' he asked as he pulled a notebook and pen from an inside jacket pocket.

Caitlin thought for a moment. "It must have been around five this evening. I'd gone for a walk, and it was almost dark. Of course, with the storm, it's hard to tell from the light, but I think it was close to five.''

Deputy Schroeder checked his notebook. "Yes. The dispatcher logged your call at five-seventeen. How far away was this vehicle?''

Caitlin walked to the door and pointed through the window. "About three miles across there.''

The deputy looked, then asked, "Is there any access to the land, or would he have had to cut the fence?''

"No, there's a gate. It's locked, though, so he'd have to cut the lock. I have the only key."

He made another note. "I'll drive out and take a look, but I don't think I'll find anything in this storm."

"Thanks," Caitlin said. "I hate to bother you, but I feel better knowing that the sheriff's department is aware of the problem."

"I should be back in half an hour or so," Schroeder said. "At least I can let you know if you need a new lock." He smiled and put his Stetson back on as he left.

The minutes dragged as Caitlin puttered in the kitchen, brewing a pot of coffee and putting some leftover sweet rolls in the oven to heat. The least she could offer him was something hot in exchange for his help at this time of night. Heavens! It was already a quarter to twelve.

Deputy Schroeder knocked, and she hurried to let him in. He whacked his hat against his leg to knock the snow off and came into the kitchen. "Looks like you'll have to get a new padlock for that gate. Someone cut it, all right," he said, holding up the lock in a plastic bag.

"But who?" Caitlin wondered.

He shrugged and accepted the steaming cup of coffee that she handed him. "Thanks. I couldn't see much. There's been too much snow to locate any tracks. I kicked the lock out of a drift beside the gate. At least he had the decency to close the gate behind himself." In ranching country it was a cardinal sin to leave any gate open, whether there was livestock in the pasture or not.

Caitlin sat down at the table and gestured for the deputy to pull up a chair.

"Now what?" she asked.

"I'll take the lock into town and file a report. There's not much else I can do." He shrugged and smiled at her, indicating his helplessness in the face of time delay, snow, and lack of evidence. Wreaths of steam curled from his cup as he sipped the hot coffee.

Caitlin slid the plate of cinnamon rolls across the table, and he took one.

"Thanks," he said. "It's been a long shift. This'll hold me until I get back to town. Can you think of any reason for someone to be trespassing in the middle of a storm?"

"It's certainly puzzling," she mused. "There's nothing out there except forest and pasture. I can't think of anything that would attract visitors. Obviously the person wasn't lost. No one would cut a padlock to try to find his way to the nearest house or road. I'd better buy a new lock tomorrow. Or several." She sipped reflectively at her coffee.

He laughed. "Maybe you can get a better deal if you buy them in bulk."

She smiled, too. "I hope I don't need that many, but I can't be running to town all the time. I'd better get at least a couple." She sobered. "Seriously, do you think there's any danger? I'm here alone with two teenagers."

He shook his head. "I doubt it. They took the trouble to stay as far from the house as they could. If someone doesn't want to be seen, that usually means they won't be bothering people."

"That's true," she agreed. "I'll try not to worry about it."

"Thanks for the coffee and roll," he said as he rose.

"You're welcome. Thanks for coming out so late."

"That's what I get paid for," he said as he left.

Caitlin moved quietly through the downstairs rooms, making sure that all the locks were fastened. At each window she peered into the darkness, alert for anything out of the ordinary, but all she saw was the thickly falling snow.

It was a strange feeling, making herself a prisoner. The house was seldom locked, and she resented the trespasser who had made her feel unsafe in her own home.

As she climbed the stairs to go to bed, her thoughts lingered on the trespasser. Was he still around? Would he come back? And most important, what did he want?

Chapter Seven

"**I** want you both to be extra careful," Caitlin admonished Linnie and Jeff as she dished up scrambled eggs and sausage the next morning. "Whoever was out in the pasture cut the lock to get in. The deputy didn't think there's much danger, but I don't want you to take any chances, okay?"

"Sure," Jeff said as he buttered a second slice of toast. "What do you suppose anyone would want in the north pasture?"

"I don't have any idea," Caitlin said, "but if I catch them, they'll wish they'd trespassed somewhere else." She slammed the platter down on the table.

"Take it easy," Linnie said. "Maybe it was just kids. You know, Saturday night and nothing to do?"

"Joyriding in a snowstorm? I doubt it." Caitlin looked skeptical. "But there's nothing we can do about it now, so let's forget it."

"Are we going to church this morning?" Jeff asked.

"Yes, and we'd better start getting ready," Caitlin replied. "We'll leave the dishes until after we get back. And I want to pick up another padlock for the north gate."

As they took their usual seats in the polished wooden pew, Caitlin surrendered her uneasy feeling and relaxed into the age-old ritual that always comforted her. The high, arched windows on either side of the church shone in rainbow colors, and the familiar hymns drifted over the congregation. Pots of snowy lilies flanked the altar and scented the air. Reverend Dimmock spoke of the coming Easter season, and reminded the congregation that life eternal awaited those who believed in Jesus. Caitlin wondered, not for the first time, about Heaven, and if her parents were safe. They must be, she assured herself, because they were so good. God must have wanted them badly to have taken them so soon. The familiar lump filled her throat, but her eyes remained dry. *I must be getting used to it,* she thought. It seemed like years since they had died, not weeks. So much had required her attention that she hadn't had time to wallow in her misery. Maybe that was what people meant when they said time heals all wounds.

After the service, the family gathered on the steps outside the church. In the way of March, the weather had once more changed, and the sun shone warmly from a cloudless sky. The old brick walls of the church glowed in the light, and Caitlin soaked in the warmth. Most of the worshipers had shed their coats and jackets, and stood around chatting.

"Caitlin! Good to see you again." Ed Bauer shook hands with her. The old rancher's single concession to Sunday was to wear his clean, silverbelly Stetson instead of his battered, everyday black cowboy hat, but Caitlin knew that his heart, not his dress code, assured him of a place in heaven, and she returned his hearty greeting. "We missed you the last couple of Sundays," he continued.

She wrinkled her nose and said, "I know. What with

finishing up the quarter at school and everything else that's happened, we just didn't have the time.''

''I know what you mean,'' Ed said.

''By the way, thanks for coming to our rescue the night of the funeral. I didn't want to talk to Tony, and Mae said you practically had to drag him out.'' Her expression made it abundantly clear what she thought of Tony's behavior that night.

Ed frowned and rubbed his cheek. ''He sure was persistent. I hope he hasn't been bothering you.''

Caitlin looked at Linnie and Jeff, and all three giggled.

''Did I say something funny?'' Ed asked.

''Well, I don't know if you'd exactly call it being bothered, but Tony asked me to marry him yesterday.''

''What? What did you tell him?'' Ed scowled. He looked as if he'd like to throttle Tony.

''Oh, I said no, of course,'' Caitlin replied, thus saving Tony from Ed's wrath. ''We have our own plans for the future, and right now that doesn't include marriage for any of us. Right, guys?''

Jeff had to tease. ''I don't know. Linnie's had an awful crush on Ben Huseman.''

''I have not!'' Linnie blushed and punched her brother's arm.

''Children!'' Caitlin said severely, and they subsided.

''So what are your plans?'' Ed asked.

Caitlin explained their idea of converting the old barn to a bed-and-breakfast as the other two drifted off to join their friends.

''It sounds like you have your work cut out for you,'' Ed said when she'd finished. ''Are you sure this thing will work?''

''It has to.'' Caitlin spoke quietly but forcefully.

"We're not selling the ranch, and we're not leaving. That's home, and it's where the Morriseys belong."

Ed shook his head. "I admire your pluck. If there's anything I can do to help, let me know. And the rest, too." His gesture included all their friends and neighbors. "You kids aren't alone, you know. We thought the world of your folks, and we'd do anything to help their kids."

"Thanks, Ed," she said. "By the way, do you know anyone who's in the market for machinery? We have all the stuff in the old barn that we don't use anymore. Most of it still works."

He rubbed his chin thoughtfully. "I don't know right offhand, but you could put an ad in the paper and have a sale. Maybe some of those antique dealers, like Maxine James, might be interested in what you've got."

"That's a great idea," she said. "I'll call the paper first thing tomorrow."

"I'd better go," Ed said. "I see Mel waiting. We're going out to lunch." He slipped his jacket back on and got into his neighbor's car.

"See you." Caitlin waved as they pulled away from the curb. Then she went to find Linnie and Jeff.

They stopped at the discount store at the edge of town. "I'll just be a minute," Caitlin said. "I just need a couple of padlocks. Why don't you wait here?"

"How about if I run over to Burger King and get us some lunch?" Jeff asked.

Caitlin thought of their dwindling checkbook balance, then relented. "Okay. I'll have a cheeseburger, some fries, and a chocolate shake. Here's a twenty."

Jeff and Linnie ran across the road, and Caitlin went into the huge K Mart store. The aisles were crowded, and she eased her way through the throng to the hardware department. The lock she wanted hung high on the wall, and she stretched to reach it. Suddenly a hand came from behind her and lifted it off the hook. She turned to face Connor Devlin.

His face was as grim as it had been the day he came to try to buy the ranch. She wondered if he ever smiled.

"I see you're having a little trouble," he said as he held the lock out to her. For a moment she wondered how he could have known about the trespasser, then realized he was referring to her height.

"Yes. Thank you." Her hand brushed his as she reached for the lock, and a tingle ran up her arm. She snatched the lock and turned away, but he grasped her shoulder. The warmth of his hand penetrated her thin blouse, and she shivered under his touch.

"I'm sorry I appeared to be harassing you the other day," he said. His voice was deep and smoky, like tattered velvet. "I didn't mean to upset you. I'm just not a very patient person. I thought I could help you out while I got something I needed and wanted."

"I understand." Her voice was cold as she pulled away from him. "Your timing was lousy, but anytime you try to buy the ranch will be just as lousy. I'm not selling. Good-bye." She marched down the aisle, shouldering her way past the browsers, completely forgetting that she'd meant to buy two locks. As she stood in line at the express lane, she felt him behind her, but she refused to turn, and he didn't speak again.

As soon as she'd paid for the lock, she hurried out to the car. Jeff and Linnie were still across the highway at Burger King, so she pulled across into the restaurant parking lot. She beeped the horn as Jeff backed out the door, his hands full of bags and cups. Linnie opened the car door so he could slide in.

"That smells wonderful," Caitlin said as she reached for the sack Jeff was struggling with.

Linnie handed Caitlin her shake and dug through one of the bags for the cheeseburger and fries. They sat in the sunny parking lot, enjoying their first taste of fast food in weeks.

"I'd forgotten how good food is when someone else cooks it," Linnie said.

"You've really helped out in the kitchen," Caitlin said. "I promise I'll try to do more."

"That's okay," Linnie replied. "I don't mind cooking as long as you guys do the dishes."

Jeff groaned. "Let's buy lots of paper plates."

Linnie and Jeff chattered most of the way home, and Caitlin tried to pay attention and block out the memory of how Connor Devlin's touch made her pulse race. It was ridiculous. It was his fault her parents were dead. How could she be attracted to him? But a niggling doubt remained. What if someone *had* let the fence down, as he claimed? What if it wasn't his fault?

She swerved violently as the thought struck her . . . what if her parents' deaths hadn't been an accident?

"Hey, watch what you're doing," Jeff shouted. "You almost went in the ditch!" He brushed at the Coke that had spattered his jacket.

"Sorry," Caitlin muttered. She couldn't voice her suspicions to the others. She could hardly believe it herself. No, it was too fantastic. Of course it was an accident. It had to be. No one would want to see her folks dead.

Would they?

Chapter Eight

"So you see, Mr. Faraday, there's a growing trend toward more personalized vacations. People want to get away from the crowds and make contact with real people again. I think . . . no, I *know* this will work." Caitlin leaned across the loan officer's desk and tapped her finger on the stack of documentation she had presented him.

"I have to agree, Miss Morrisey. You've done your homework." Mr. Faraday smiled. "I think we can loan you twenty thousand on a five-year note. We'll even make the first payment due the end of July. That'll give you a chance to make the payment when the guests start rolling in."

"Thank you," she said. Her heart thudded, and she hoped he didn't notice the tremor in her hands.

"Do you want this deposited to your ranch account?" he asked.

"No, I'd like to keep the business separate from the ranch expenses. It'll be easier to keep track of that way." She wanted to leap and shout and dance him around the bank, but she only smiled beatifically.

"Of course," he said. "However you want to do it. I'll get the forms." He punched some information into his computer. The printer hummed and the loan papers rolled out, ready for her signature.

Mr. Faraday explained the terms and pointed to the

signature line. Caitlin signed the papers and accepted her book of temporary checks.

"Thank you," she said as she stood to go. "I don't think you'll be sorry."

"I'm sure I won't," he replied.

The sun poured down warm and yellow, and she drew deep breaths of almost-spring air as she walked across the parking lot. The snow was gone now, except in the north-facing, shaded places. There was a freshness in the air, a scent of newness, and it exhilarated her.

Cattle trucks had arrived at the ranch yesterday morning, and the herd was on its way to the new owner. The broker had told her a check would be arriving in a few days. She felt light and free from worry for the first time in weeks.

She stopped at the pay phone on the corner and called Richard Jones's office.

"Miss Morrisey, good to hear from you," Richard said.

"Please call me Cait," she replied. "After all, we're going to be spending a lot of time together."

"You got the loan?" She heard the excitement in his voice.

"I sure did, thanks to your suggestions and calculations. Now can you tell me how to reach this friend of yours, the architect?"

"Talk about coincidence," Richard replied. "He's standing right here. In fact, we were just talking about your project. He's really excited about it. Hold on. Here he is."

"Hi. This is Peter Northrup. Miss Morrisey?" His voice was almost childlike, but he sounded enthusiastic.

"Yes," Caitlin answered. "Has Richard told you what I have in mind?"

"We were just discussing it. It sounds like a great project. I'm looking forward to working with you."

"When can we get together?" Caitlin asked. "I'd like to get started as soon as possible."

"How about this afternoon? If you meet me here, I can follow you out to your place and look it over," he said.

"Wonderful!" she exclaimed. "I'll be there in a few minutes."

Peter Northrup turned out to be a rather chubby young man, already tending toward baldness. But his bright blue eyes and cheerful face enchanted Caitlin at once. He reminded her of an elf in a children's story she'd read years ago.

"So glad to meet you," he said, pumping her hand.

"Me too," Caitlin replied. "Richard tells me he's very impressed with your work."

"Great! Great! I can use all the good press I can get," he said. "Let's get started." He bounced on the balls of his feet. Caitlin expected him to balloon toward the ceiling at any instant. They shook hands with Richard Jones and got into their respective vehicles.

Caitlin drove out of town, glad that she was in the lead. Peter's driving seemed to be as enthusiastic as the rest of him. When they reached the ranch, she pulled up in front of the old barn, and Northrup splashed to a stop beside her. He jumped out, ignoring the puddles of water left by the snowmelt.

"Oh, yes," he said, looking the building over. "It has possibilities, definite possibilities."

She pushed the door open, and he blinked rapidly as his eyes adjusted to the gloomy interior of the barn.

Caitlin caught his arm and steadied him when he tripped over an old wagon tongue.

She started to explain what she had in mind, but he was way ahead of her. "One big suite in the loft—two bedrooms and a bath. Then underneath, two separate rooms with private baths. And then if we put the communal kitchen sink right here, all the plumbing will be centralized, minimizing problems. And bookcases there. And big windows, there and there, to really open up the space."

He whipped out a notebook and tape measure and made his way through the tangle of machinery, murmuring to himself, ignoring Caitlin, lost in thoughts of creating the perfect guesthouse.

"I have to start dinner," Caitlin said. "Come on up to the house when you're finished."

He waved absently and went on with his calculations.

Caitlin went into the house and put a chicken and some potatoes in the oven to bake. The odor of roasting meat permeated the house by the time Peter Northrup appeared, dusty and rumpled from his foray in the barn.

"I'm so glad you called me in for this," he said, accepting the cup of tea she offered. "I've been wanting to do a renovation like this. In fact, I'd be willing to lower my fee if I can take pictures and use this place as an example for an article for a professional journal."

"Gosh, that's great! Feel free to do whatever you'd like. How soon can we get started?" Caitlin asked as she joined him at the table.

He said, "I'll have the plans drawn up by the end of the week. After that, it's all up to Richard."

"Things are falling into place better than I ever dreamed," she said.

"I believe in serendipity," he said as he stood up. "Now I'd better get going. I can't wait to get started on the plans." He patted his shirt pocket to make sure his notebook was safe. "Yes, I've got all the measurements."

Caitlin stood in the late-afternoon sun and waved as he drove away. Another car slowed and turned into the lane as Peter pulled onto the main road, and she stifled a groan as she recognized Tony's vehicle.

"Hi, Cait. Who was that?" Tony asked as he got out. He was dressed as if for a social occasion, not like a working rancher, and Caitlin wondered how he managed to keep his spread working, since he never seemed to supervise it or do any work himself.

"Just the architect," she replied shortly, turning to go into the house. "Come on in," she added grudgingly.

Tony frowned as he followed her into the kitchen. He tossed his black Stetson onto the kitchen table. "So you're determined to go ahead with this cockeyed scheme," he said.

Caitlin bent over the stove and fiddled with the chicken, turning and basting it so she wouldn't have to look at him.

"It's not cockeyed," she said shortly. "I have the loan, the architect, and the construction company. They all seem to think I can do it. I don't know why you're so negative." She slammed the lid back on the roaster and shoved it into the oven.

Her face was flushed from the heat of the oven—or from vexation—when she turned to face him, and the breeze had ruffled her short, dark hair into curls around her face.

"Oh, Cait." Tony reached for her and pulled her to him, holding her hard while his lips sought hers.

Aghast, she struggled, twisting her head so that his kiss brushed her cheek. He held her even tighter, trying again to capture her lips. "Come on, Cait. I love you," he whispered.

"Stop it!" Caitlin screamed. "Let me go, now!" She shoved hard, and he staggered back against the table. She stood panting, her arm raised to strike, a wooden spoon for a weapon. "How dare you! How dare you!" She was so incensed that she lost the power of speech.

Tony straightened up. "Cait, I'm sorry. I just lost control." He held out his hands, pleading. "It's just that you're so beautiful. I promise I won't do it again. Please forgive me, Cait. Please?"

Slowly she lowered the spoon. Her eyes sparked, and she pointed a finger at him for emphasis. "Don't you *ever* touch me like that again," she warned.

"I won't. I promise." Tony hung his head and stuck his hands in his pockets. He looked just like a little boy who'd been caught in the cookie jar.

That's exactly how he wants me to see him, Caitlin thought. *His little-kid act. It won't work this time.*

"It's time you left," she said. "I have dinner to fix, and I don't have time for this nonsense."

"Wait. That's not what I came out here for," he said.

"Well? What did you want?" Caitlin crossed her arms and leaned against the counter, the spoon still in her hand.

Tony sat down at the table and folded his hands in front of him, giving Caitlin a rueful smile.

"I really came out to make you a business offer," he said. "I know you're hard up, and I thought I'd offer to buy the ranch. You may not know it, but I've been planning to expand my operation."

"No," she said.

"Well, how could you know, being away at school so much?" He tapped the tabletop with a forefinger. "You bet I'm expanding. Soon I'll be a bigger rancher than Connor Devlin ever thought of being." A fleeting expression of hatred crossed his face, only for a second; then he regained control.

"I meant no, I'm not selling you the ranch," Caitlin explained. "I'm not selling to anyone, not you, not Connor Devlin, not the Devil himself."

Tony jumped up. "You mean Devlin's already tried to buy the place? Why, that double-dealing—"

Caitlin broke in, her tone sarcastic. "He only did what you just tried to do. At least he didn't tell me he loved me, the way you did." She gazed steadily at him, and he, embarrassed, couldn't meet her eyes.

He shifted uncomfortably and ran a hand through his hair. "But I *do* love you, Cait. You know I've loved you for years. Besides, with our combined range, we could have the largest cattle operation in the county. Heck, we could *own* the county." His voice was excited now, his discomfiture gone. His face glowed with ambition and she took a step back. This was a Tony she'd not seen before, one who would do anything to achieve his aims.

"I'm not interested in owning the county," she snapped, concealing her dismay. "Now leave. I'm extremely tired of this conversation." She folded her arms and frowned at him.

His zealous look faded and he shrugged into his coat. "Okay, I'm going. But I'll be back. Sooner or later you'll realize how you really feel about me, and you'll make me a very happy man." Tony buttoned his jacket and turned to go.

Caitlin stood silently while he let himself out, torn between laughing at his incredible ego and throwing the chicken at his head. Fortunately for Jeff and Linnie, laughter won out and dinner was saved.

She decided not to mention the incident to her brother and sister. They had enough on their minds without worrying about her and Tony.

Linnie and Jeff were as excited as kids around a Christmas tree when they found out the loan had been approved. Caitlin had set the table, and Jeff was shuttling food from the stove to the table.

"We'd better get the barn cleaned out so they can start work," Jeff said as he set the roast chicken down on a hot pad. "I'll even stay home from school tomorrow and help you." His eagerness to help didn't fool her for a minute.

"Thanks, but you've got that math test, remember?" Caitlin could tell from his expression that the math test was the reason he'd volunteered to stay home and help.

"Besides," she added, "I put an ad in the paper today. It'll start tomorrow morning. We're having a barn sale on Saturday. You can both help then. Whatever we don't sell, we'll store in the new barn. But there's no point in moving all that stuff. Let the buyers move it." They sat down, and Caitlin passed the chicken to Linnie.

"How will we know what to charge?" Jeff asked as he cut into his baked potato and smeared it with fresh butter.

"I hope that people will be honest and offer what it's worth," Caitlin said, "but if an offer sounds too low, I'll just refuse it. But keep in mind that the purpose of the sale isn't to make a fortune. It's to get the barn cleaned out so we can go ahead with our plans."

"Yeah," Jeff said, "but a few hundred extra dollars sure wouldn't hurt anything."

"You're right about that," Caitlin agreed. "The money from the loan has to be used only for construction and operation expenses. Any personal expenses have to come out of what's left in the ranch account and what we get from the sale."

"Are we incredibly broke?" Linnie asked. Her forehead creased with worry as she stared at her older sister.

"Let's put it this way," Caitlin said. Her tone was light, but there was an underlying seriousness in her speech. "We're walking a very thin line between poor and poverty-stricken. There aren't going to be any extras for a while. Last month's electric bill took a big chunk out of what we have left."

They finished the meal in silence, each dwelling on thoughts of how to conserve or earn more. The mood was as dark as the evening sky.

"I guess I'll go up and study," Jeff said as he pushed back his chair and went to stack his dishes in the sink.

"Me too," Linnie said as she followed him.

Caitlin let them go. She didn't mind doing the dishes and having time alone with her thoughts. Tony had almost convinced her with his poor-little-me act, but she couldn't shake the feeling that there was something besides love behind his proposal. He wanted the land badly, and if he couldn't buy it or marry it, what were his options? She racked her brain, trying to think of any other way he could get his hands on the ranch, but couldn't think of any. Unless, of course, her plan of offering western hospitality failed, and the bank foreclosed.

"No!" she said aloud. "It's our home. We'll stay no matter what."

She turned off the kitchen light and made her way upstairs, unaware that dark forces were already gathering to defeat her.

Chapter Nine

March segued into April and then into May, but Caitlin was too busy to notice the change from harsh winter to tentative spring. The barn sale had gone well, bringing in a little over two thousand dollars. She'd saved a few old plowshares, a doubletree from some long-forgotten ox team, and some wagon wheels to use for decoration when the guesthouse was finished.

The construction crew had arrived in the middle of March, and she'd spent every waking moment consulting with Richard on bathroom and lighting fixtures, and figuring the best way to heat the rooms. Richard's advice was invaluable.

"See, if we put in a separate water heater with a closed system, you can heat the rooms with hot-water baseboard heat. It's even and clean, and you won't have to worry about power outages, since it'll be run from the propane tank."

Caitlin agreed. She'd toyed with the idea of a fireplace or woodstove, but her insurance premiums would have skyrocketed. If the guests wanted a fire, they'd just have to settle for one in the barbecue pit being built outside.

The printer had finished the brochures, and they were perfect, with Caitlin's delicate line drawing showing the guesthouse as it would look when it was finished. Linnie had proved her literary talent with the wording. Anyone seeing the brochure would certainly think about staying at Spring Hollow Guest Ranch.

Jeff had come up with the name unintentionally. They had racked their brains for weeks, trying to come up with a name, and one afternoon, as they'd walked across the ranch yard, Jeff had gazed off across the pasture toward the mountains looming to the west. "You know," he had said, "a great trail ride would be up into the hills where that little spring comes out of the hollow, at the foot of Storm King Mountain. The water's pure, and it'd be a perfect place for lunch."

"That's it!" Caitlin had shouted as she grabbed her brother and hugged him. "Spring Hollow. How's that for a name for our enterprise?"

"Spring Hollow," Linnie mused. "I like it. It makes me feel relaxed just saying it. I vote for it."

"Me too," Jeff had said, looking pleased at his sisters' praise. "I could ask my shop teacher if I could make a sign to go over the lane out by the road. We have to do some kind of woodworking project before the year's over. If you'd lay out the lettering, Cait, I could rout it and stain it. It'd be great! Everyone would know right away that they'd found us."

"What a wonderful idea," Linnie had said.

"I agree," Caitlin had added. "Give me some measurements, and I'll call the lumberyard tomorrow. You can pick up the stuff on your way to school."

Now Caitlin stood, hands on hips, looking over the project. A new propane tank had been installed behind the old barn. It would heat the water and fuel the gas range. Latticework disguised its silver bulk, and Caitlin could picture morning glories twining up the woven wood to hide it even further. The barbecue pit was done, looking as if it had always sat there under the old cottonwood. The lines leading to the septic tank had been covered over and grass seed sprinkled over the raw earth. Soon the creeping greenness of spring would hide the scars completely.

The only thing left to do was to furnish the building. Caitlin had ordered new beds and mattresses from the furniture store in town, and the linens and curtains had come from a mail-order company. During the sale, several old oak chairs had been unearthed, and Linnie had spent the last month refinishing them. With a couple of couches, an armchair or two, and a dining table, the common room would be complete.

Caitlin went to town early Wednesday morning and prowled through the secondhand stores. She'd also circled several ads in the paper that advertised furniture for sale. She found two dressers at the Nifty Thrifty Store that would fit perfectly in the two smaller bedrooms. The Bargain Den yielded a couch and matching armchair upholstered in a soft floral fabric.

After making arrangements to pick up the furniture later, she looked over the ads. The most promising one appeared to be a yard sale on the east end of town.

The lilacs of early May spread purple and white blossoms in every yard, and tulips and daffodils sprouted from neat flower beds. As she drove through the quiet streets, enjoying the spring weather, she thought how lucky she was to have everything going so well. Tony hadn't been around much since he'd tried to kiss her in the kitchen. In fact, she'd seen him only a few times in passing. She'd been so busy with the construction and other details that she hadn't really stopped to wonder why he hadn't followed up on his promise to come back and propose again.

The sale wasn't difficult to spot. Furniture, appliances,

clothing, and miscellaneous items filled the yard of a two-story blue house in the middle of the block. Caitlin eased the truck into a parking space several doors down and walked back to join the people browsing through the collection.

A round oak table was almost buried under a load of games, books, and small appliances. It would be perfect for the dining table in the common room.

Caitlin found the person in charge, a tall man, thin and stooped with age.

"Yep. Too big a place to take care of by myself. Gonna move into an apartment over there in the retirement village. I hate to see it go, but I sure don't have room for it all." The woman he was speaking to sympathized, paid for the corner shelf she'd picked out, and left.

Caitlin asked the price of the dining table.

"Well, let's see. It's pretty old, almost as old as I am." He wheezed out a chuckle. "Had it down in the basement for years. It needs some gluing, so I'll let you have it for, oh, thirty dollars."

"That sounds fair," Caitlin said, nodding. "Do you happen to have a coffee table?"

"Let me see." The old man rubbed his chin and turned slowly in a circle, surveying the collection. "Yep. Right over there." He led the way to a mound of bric-a-brac that hid an oval cherry wood table with a glass top. "Now, that's in pretty good shape. I'd like to have about fifty for that."

Caitlin bit her lip, doing quick calculations in her head, then agreed. "Here's eighty dollars. Is there anyone around who can help me load them?" She handed him three twenties and two tens from the slim bundle of bills in her pocket.

The old man shook his head doubtfully. "I'm the only one, and I'm not too spry. But tell you what. Back into the driveway. Then you won't have to carry them so far."

Caitlin carefully maneuvered the truck backward down the street and swung into the driveway. The old man had cleaned the paraphernalia off each table and stood by to help as much as possible. He and Caitlin slid the big dining table across the lawn, but he couldn't help her lift it because of his back trouble. He went to help some new customers, and she wished she'd had sense enough to bring Jeff with her, even if it meant he would miss a morning of school.

She sighed and squatted under the table, straightening to lift two legs off the ground and onto the tailgate of the truck. Unfortunately, she couldn't let go or the whole thing would slide right back out of the truck.

"Oh, darn!" she muttered.

Suddenly the weight of the table lifted off her back, and the table slid easily into the truck. She turned to find Connor Devlin standing behind her.

"In trouble again, I see," he said. He still didn't smile, but there was a suspicion of a twinkle in his gray eyes.

Flustered, Caitlin wiped her palms on her jeans. "I just . . ." She gestured to the truck. "I guess I'm not tall enough. Thank you."

"You're welcome."

She strode across the lawn to the smaller coffee table and hoisted it, straining back to balance the weight. Devlin started toward her, and she desperately tried to think of some way to avoid his help.

"Hey, Cait! What're you doing hauling furniture?"

"Ed! How nice to see you again." Caitlin set the table down and massaged the small of her back. To her relief,

Connor Devlin swerved away and began to rummage through the pile of board games in one corner of the yard.

"The guest house is finished. I'm just picking up a few things to furnish it," she explained. "I've got these tables, and some dressers and a couch and chair at a couple of shops downtown. I don't think I'll be able to get everything in one load. I guess I'll have to make another trip tomorrow." She sighed at the prospect of spending another morning away from the ranch when there was so much still to be done.

The older man said, "I'll tell you what. I'll bring them out for you, but I won't be able to make it until Saturday. I'll just hitch up that old wood-hauling trailer of mine. The furniture should fit fine. Anything else you need hauled?"

Caitlin said, "Thanks so much, Ed. There are still a couple of mattresses and box springs that were shipped late. If they're in by Saturday, you could pick them up at Sullivan's. I'll call and tell them to let you have them."

"Okay." Ed Bauer stooped and lifted the coffee table easily. "I'll put this in the truck for you. Do you want the glass up front?"

"I suppose it would be safer on the seat," she agreed.

She thanked Ed for his help and put the truck in gear. As she pulled out of the driveway, she saw Connor Devlin paying for a stack of games and wondered vaguely who he had to play games with. Since he'd bought the place a year ago, he'd lived alone, except for the ranch hands, on the ranch to the west of hers. He'd kept to himself, almost a crime in the close-knit western community. For a while, people had speculated on why he had bought the biggest spread around, but even his hired hands couldn't shed much light on his elusive character.

He paid them well and kept to himself, so Saturday-night saloon conversations couldn't satisfy the town's curiosity. Soon the neighboring ranchers had left him to his eccentricity and gone on about their business.

Back at the ranch, she unloaded the smaller items, but left the larger table for Jeff to move when he got home. She changed from jeans into shorts and a summery blouse. The sky spread, cobalt and cloudless, over the valley, propped up at the edges by the mountains. She stood for a moment, breathing the sweet May air that carried the scent of wildflowers and new grass. The snow line on the mountains receded every day, and soon only the very tops would be tipped with white. The petunias and pansies she'd set out in the new flower beds around the old barn swayed in the breeze. The sun caressed her skin, driving out the last remnant of winter's chill.

She gathered up her gardening tools and seed packets and knelt in the garden plot that Jeff had prepared over the weekend. The familiar musty odor of the newly turned earth took her back to long-ago springs when she'd helped her mother plant the vegetables that would grace their summer dinner table and fill the pantry shelves come autumn. She hummed as she dug the furrows and dropped seeds and covered them. She lost all track of time and was startled to see the shadows lengthening as the sun dropped toward the western horizon.

Caitlin straightened up, bending and twisting to take the kinks out of her back. She sauntered across the barnyard, savoring the golden glow of the late-afternoon sunlight. This was her favorite time of day, the time when work was done and she could sink into the peacefulness of the approaching evening. The pasture grass tickled her bare legs as she slipped between the corral poles. Rough and Ready grazed far out in the field, their chestnut coats gleaming in the slanting rays of the lowering sun. Caitlin strolled along, letting her thoughts wander and stopping to pick wild iris and purple penstemon that grew everywhere. When she'd gathered a large bouquet, she walked back to the house, arriving just as Linnie and Jeff drove up.

"Hi. Would you two like to go to the cemetery with me?" she asked, keeping her voice steady. "I've got some flowers to take."

Jeff and Linnie were silent for a moment. None of them had been to their parents' graves since the funeral. At first they'd been reluctant to go, not wanting to be reminded of the tragedy. Then they'd been too busy with the plans for the guest house.

"Sure," Linnie said, looking at her brother for confirmation. Jeff nodded.

"Fine. Let me change real quick," Caitlin said as she followed them into the house. She found a large, empty canning jar and filled it with water and arranged the flowers in it. Then she ran upstairs and changed into jeans and a long-sleeved chambray shirt.

Linnie had also changed into jeans, and the three climbed into the cab of the truck. The sun hovered low in the sky as they drove up the meandering dirt road to the cemetery. Jeff shifted restlessly, and Linnie picked at a drooping iris in the bouquet. Caitlin drove, not speaking, lost in her own thoughts.

She was sad, and slightly guilty about not coming before this, but none of them had been ready to face the new headstones that had been put into place last month. Caitlin still had moments, when she was caught in that half dreamworld as she wakened in the morning, when she thought it had all been a mistake, and Mother was downstairs fixing eggs and pancakes. Then she would realize that no one was in the kitchen and nothing would get cooked until she cooked it herself.

She eased the truck to a stop at the side of the road, and they walked slowly toward the twin graves. The raw earth of February had healed with grass planted by the funeral staff, and it lay green in the long shadows of the early May evening.

The three stood awkwardly for a moment, silent in renewed grief. Then Linnie knelt to place the jar of flowers in front of the headstones, between the graves. The blooms dipped in the breeze, bridging the gap between the names, connecting their mother and father with a blush of lavender.

For a moment there was no pain, no sadness, just a hushed timelessness. Then the evening seemed to tremble as memories overwhelmed them. Caitlin wiped her eyes on her sleeve, and Jeff's jaw quivered slightly as he reached for his handkerchief. Linnie sat bowed over, her hand resting lightly on her mother's grave.

Caitlin spoke first. "It's sure different from the last time we were here."

"A lot warmer," Jeff said, his voice husky with tears.

"And a lot friendlier," Linnie added. "They're together forever. It's peaceful somehow. I'm glad we came. I'd rather remember the grass and flowers than mud and snow."

"Me too," her brother agreed.

Caitlin said quietly, "It still hurts, and I guess it always will, but it's easier now. I feel like they're at rest, not just dead." Linnie patted her mother's grave one last time and rose to her feet. The three stood silently as the last rays of the sun dipped behind the peaks, and a twilight chill settled across the land. Then they hurried back to the truck, glad to be out of the evening wind that rolled off the mountains.

The road home passed the gate to the north pasture. Caitlin pulled over in the gathering dusk, and Jeff jumped out to check the padlock, something he did quite regularly now.

"It's okay," he called as he tugged at the lock.

"Good," Caitlin said. She put the truck in gear and they drove on through the twilight.

"I'm glad we haven't had any more trespassers," Linnie said. "I thought all along it was kids. I guess I was right."

Caitlin frowned. "I'm not so sure about it being kids, but I'm glad there haven't been any more mysterious lights."

Jeff spoke up. "Did the sheriff ever find out anything about the lock?"

Caitlin shook her head. "No fingerprints, nothing. But they didn't really expect to, what with the lock being covered by snow and the fact that any sane person would be wearing gloves in the middle of a blizzard."

"Then do we have to keep checking the lock?" he asked. "It's kind of a pain coming out here every day or so."

"I guess not," she said reluctantly, "but keep an eye out for any lights. Or anything else out of the ordinary."

They pulled up next to the old barn, and Jeff and Caitlin hauled the large table into the guesthouse.

"What a great table," Jeff said as soon as it was set in place under the large window that had been installed in the west wall of the old barn. "It's a little shaky, though." He rocked it with one hand.

"The man I bought it from said it needed gluing," his sister said.

Linnie pulled the chairs she'd refinished into place around it. "Look. They're almost perfect matches," she exclaimed.

"And I found a couch and chair and some dressers for the two downstairs rooms," Caitlin continued. "Ed Bauer's bringing them out Saturday, along with the mattresses that were back ordered."

"Hey, hey, we're doin' okay!" Jeff shouted. "All set to go, two weeks early."

"That reminds me," Caitlin said. "We need to put a bunch of brochures out around town. Art said we could put some at the Quik-Stop, and the chamber of commerce has room for some in their office. Would you take care of that Friday, Linnie?"

"Sure. I'll do it during lunch."

Caitlin put one hand on her stomach to quiet the sudden butterflies that fluttered there. This was it. In three days they would be officially open. What would the summer bring? Only time would tell.

Chapter Ten

Saturday dawned cool and damp, and the threat of rain hung in the clouds that covered the western sky.

"I hope Ed brings those things out soon," Caitlin commented as she peered through the kitchen curtains at the dark clouds curling down to hide the peaks.

"Yeah. I'd like to get the sign hung, too," Jeff said. The sign lay propped up against the kitchen wall, taking up a lot of space. Jeff caressed the smooth, polished edge and traced the letters that were carved deeply into the redwood. "I've got the eyebolts screwed into the cross-piece. I just need some help getting it up."

"I'm sure Ed will be glad to help, if it's not pouring rain," Caitlin said. The entrance to the lane was framed by two upright logs that held another log notched across the top to form a gateway of sorts. Everything was ready for the final hanging.

"It's going to look super," Linnie said. "You did a really good job on it."

"When you're good, you're good," Jeff joked, but his eyes shone. "Did I tell you I got an A plus on it?"

"Only about a million times." Linnie rolled her eyes.

Jeff stuck his tongue out at her. "I think I'll go feed the chickens. At least they appreciate me." He left, only to pop back in. "I just saw Ed turn into the lane," he

96

said. "I'll be right back. Don't start without me." Then he raced toward the barn.

Caitlin pulled on her old gray work sweater. "You'd better have a jacket," she said to Linnie. As she stepped out the door, she was astonished to see not only Ed Bauer's truck and trailer, but seven or eight other vehicles pull into the yard and park near the guesthouse. Linnie and Caitlin exchanged puzzled looks as they trotted out to the parking area.

"What's going on?" Caitlin asked Ed. "What's everybody doing here?"

Ed grinned. "I told you that you kids weren't alone, and that we'd all help. Well, we're not going to let you open the place without some kind of celebration." He pointed to friends and neighbors piling out of their cars and trucks. "You just show the women where to put the food, and we men will take care of the rest."

"What's happening?" Linnie stood close behind her sister, astonished at the cavalcade.

"Here, Cait. This needs to go in the refrigerator." Mae Bricklin held out a bowl containing a dessert made primarily of whipped cream.

"Thanks, Mae," she said as she led the way up the walk to the kitchen door, "but what on earth are you all doing?" Caitlin held the door open as neighbor after neighbor trooped into the kitchen, each bearing some sort of food.

"We need the oven for this," Alma Owens said. "Put it in at three hundred and twenty-five degrees and it'll be perfect by lunchtime." A large ham filled the roasting pan she held.

Linnie hurried to carry out her directions, and then put another pot of coffee on. The kitchen filled with conversation and activity as their neighbors laid out salads, breads, and casseroles for lunch. Mae Bricklin started to leave.

"Oh, no, you don't," Caitlin said as she blocked the doorway. "Explain." She folded her arms across her chest and tried to look menacing.

"It's very simple," her godmother said, shooing her out of the way. "We're having a housewarming for your guest ranch. I saw Ed the other day, after he talked to you about bringing the furniture out, and I decided this would be a good way to show our support. Not everybody could have put the idea together as quickly as you did, Cait. You're pretty special to us."

Caitlin threw her arms around Mae and held her tightly. "Thank you. I never imagined moving furniture would turn into a party."

"Everything's under control in here," Mae said as she withdrew from Caitlin's embrace. "Let's go out and watch the men work."

The women trailed across the ranch yard to the old barn, now officially the Spring Hollow Guest Ranch. The men had unloaded the furniture and were hauling it into the remodeled barn. Jeff, back from feeding the chickens, directed them. The barn rang with the clamor of conversation and shouted directions.

"Jeff, there's a box in the backseat of my car. Run out and get it for me, will you?" Jessie Price said.

"Sure."

"I still can't believe it," Caitlin said. "I was sure we'd be putting things together until midnight."

Mae draped her arm around Caitlin's shoulders and hugged her. "That's what friends are for. If we couldn't help you raise the barn, at least we can help you finish it."

Jeff returned with a large cardboard box. "Here you go, Mrs. Price."

"Thanks, Jeff. Just put it there on the table. Cait, come here," Jessie said.

"Dishes!" Caitlin exclaimed as she peeked into the box. "I'd forgotten all about needing dishes."

"Well, if you're going to feed people, you need something to feed them on. These are some I had stuck away in the attic. They're old, but still good. No cracks or anything."

"They're beautiful." Caitlin admired the flowered borders on the dishes. "Are you sure you don't want them? Can I buy them from you?"

Jessie waved away the suggestion. "Of course not. They've been taking up space for years. I'm glad to get rid of them. And here's a set of silverware that my cousin Jane found in her basement."

"How can I ever thank you?" Caitlin asked, her voice choked.

"Forget it. You're doing me a favor by taking them off my hands," Jessie said airily.

Jeff had been hovering on the edge of the conversation. "Hey, Cait, I'm going to hang the sign now. Mr. Devlin said he'd help."

Caitlin turned to see Connor Devlin leaning against the door frame, his shoulders almost filling the space. His black hair tumbled over his forehead, and his steely eyes penetrated her soul. Her heart turned over, and she braced herself against the sudden wave of dizziness that swept over her.

"Okay, Cait?" Jeff's question broke the spell, and she turned away from that penetrating gaze, once more in control of her emotions.

"Are you sure you can handle it?" she asked.

"Oh, for cryin' out loud. I got the eyebolts in, didn't I? We can do it. Besides, Todd's here with his dad. He'll help."

"All right. Just be careful. I don't want to have to haul you, *any* of you, to the hospital."

Todd's father, Jack Wilson, approached, carrying something under his arm. "Here, Cait. Something to get the place off on the right foot." He grinned at his pun.

Caitlin unrolled the object to reveal a welcome mat designed with a border of roses and other old-fashioned flowers surrounding the words *Friends Be Here.*

"Oh, it's beautiful! Thanks, Jack." She clutched the rug to her chest and stood on tiptoe to kiss his cheek. "My friends certainly are here. And you shall have the honor of placing it." She handed the rug back to him.

"Attention, everyone," Jack called. Gradually the hubbub quieted. He took Caitlin's hand and led her out, making her stand just outside the door. With a flourish, he spread the mat on the floor and bowed low to Caitlin. As she stepped across the threshold, he announced, "I hereby declare the Spring Hollow Guest Ranch officially open."

Whistles and applause erupted, and everyone crowded close to shake Caitlin's hand and congratulate her.

She raised her hand for silence. "Thank you all. For everything. You're the best friends anyone could have. Now, let's celebrate! Ladies, bring the food over here, and we'll serve the first official meal of Spring Hollow Guest Ranch."

Soon the food was carried from the ranch house kitchen and spread out on the guesthouse dining table. People chatted and laughed as they helped themselves to lunch. They sat or stood around the room and on the steps leading to the sleeping rooms as they ate, complimenting each other on the hard work and good food.

Thunder rumbled outside, and the first drops of rain splashed against the windows as Jeff and Todd returned, scraped and dirty, but proud.

"We got her up," Jeff said, "and nobody got hurt. Well, hardly hurt," he amended as he examined a scrape on his elbow that was beginning to ooze blood.

Caitlin looked for Connor Devlin, disappointed when she couldn't see him in the crowd. "Go wash it off and put a gauze pad on it," she said. "How'd you do it?"

"I was up on the crosspiece, reaching for the sign, and I slipped. It's a good thing Mr. Devlin was up there, or I would have fallen off. He grabbed me just in time. Save me some food, okay?" He left for the house at a dead run through the increasing rain, leaving Caitlin to wonder just what had gone on out at the gate.

She was aware of Connor Devlin before she saw him. Her skin tingled, and her scalp tightened as he stood close behind her.

"You're in business." His husky voice fell softly in her ear. She turned and looked up into his rugged countenance.

"Yes, and Jeff tells me that, thanks to you, I didn't have to make a hospital run after all." Caitlin smiled calmly at him, keeping a firm grip on her emotions.

"I doubt he would have broken anything," Connor said as he reached for a sandwich. "It's not that far to the ground. But I'm glad I could be of help."

"You always seem to be helping lately," Caitlin remarked. "Have you appointed yourself our guardian angel?" She slanted a smile at him and caught a faint movement around his mouth that might have been the start of a grin.

In the past months, she'd reevaluated her outburst the day he'd offered to buy the ranch. She could no longer, in good conscience, blame him for her parents' deaths. It had been an accident, plain and simple, and remembering her accusations brought a flush to her cheeks.

"I have to tell you something," she said, taking a deep breath. "I'm sorry for the things I said the morning you came to the house. I was upset, but that didn't give me the right to blame you for something that wasn't your fault."

He shifted closer, looming over her, and she flinched at his nearness. "I understand. I was out of line, too. I should have waited longer to make my proposal."

His words startled her, because they echoed closely what Tony had said. *I have a proposal. . . .*

He looked deep into her eyes. "Is something wrong?"

She shook her head to clear the confusion. "No, I'm fine. It was just a little déjà vu."

"Good. Then we can be friends?" He held out his hand and she took it hesitantly. The shock of his touch burned all the way to her shoulder.

"Friends," she whispered.

And he smiled for the first time since she'd known him. His normally grim expression softened and widened, and his steely eyes turned sky blue.

"What are you looking at?" he asked as her expression reflected her surprise.

"Your eyes. I've never seen anyone's eyes do that before. Change colors." She stared at him, waiting for the change to happen again. His eyes stayed blue.

"They tell me that that happens occasionally," he said as he released her hand.

"Hey, Cait, guess who's here?" Jeff was back, washed and bandaged. "Tony."

"Oh, no! Do I have time to hide?" she said with a moan, but just then the door opened and Tony Black came in, dripping on the welcome mat and wiping the mud from his shoes on the first word of the motto.

"Hi, Cait. This is quite a party. How come I wasn't invited?" he said as he shook the rain off his jacket.

"Mainly because I didn't even know about it until a couple of hours ago," she said shortly. "Our neighbors got up a housewarming for the Spring Hollow Guest Ranch."

Tony looked around appreciatively. "Does this mean you're officially open?" he asked. "How about a tour?"

He casually reached between Caitlin and Connor and took a couple of oatmeal cookies from a plate.

"Sure. Do you know Connor Devlin?" Caitlin asked. "Connor, this is our neighbor to the east, Tony Black."

Tony juggled cookies to shake Connor's hand. Caitlin noticed that Connor's eyes were gunmetal gray again.

"Nice to meet you," Tony said, his perfect teeth gleaming whitely against his tanned face. "I've seen you around, but I don't think we've been introduced."

"No, we haven't," Connor said. "Excuse me. I have to get home." He touched the brim of his Stetson as a gesture of respect to Caitlin and abruptly strode away.

"Surly character, isn't he?" Tony said as they watched Connor's broad back vanish through the door. "Now how about that tour?" His smile brightened, if such a thing were possible, as he took her arm.

His grip forced Caitlin to move through the barn, showing him the two bedrooms below and the two-bedroom suite in the loft. He didn't seem to notice her lack of enthusiasm in his company.

"Say, this is really something," he said. His tone was admiring, but she caught a hint of hardness in his voice.

"I didn't believe you could actually pull it off. I have to hand it to you, Cait."

"Thanks," she said curtly. "I'd better get back to my hostess duties." She freed herself and went back downstairs.

The crowded room had cleared somewhat as people began drifting out to their cars, still talking and congratulating each other on their successful surprise party. The rain had moved off to the east, and the late-afternoon sun slanted through rifts in the purple clouds. A huge double rainbow shimmered in the sky, holding the farmhouse captive under its brilliant arch.

Cries of wonder greeted the sight, and Jack Wilson said, "It looks like you've found the pot of gold."

"Yes," Caitlin replied. "What more could I ask for in the way of omens?"

She had no way of knowing how tarnished her pot of gold would be in only a few short hours.

Chapter Eleven

"Cait! Cait!" Jeff's scream shocked Caitlin out of her dreams. She fumbled in the dark for the light switch.

"What?" she screamed back.

"The barn! Oh no, the barn!" The back door slammed open against the kitchen wall.

"Jeff! Jeff! Come back!" Caitlin scrambled down the stairs two at a time. "Linnie! Wake up!"

Caitlin flew into the yard and staggered as she saw the orange glow lighting the windows of the common room of the Spring Hollow Guest Ranch. She sprinted toward the barn as she caught sight of Jeff struggling with the door. He disappeared inside before she could reach him. Thick smoke curled into the night, and the fire blazed more brightly with the air that flowed in from the open door. Caitlin ran inside and groped through the thick, orange-tinged smoke, trying to find her brother.

"Jeff!" The cry caught in her throat as the smoke choked her. She saw him outlined against the fire, aiming the nozzle of the fire extinguisher at the base of the flames. The chemical shot out, smothering the blaze, and Jeff kept spraying until the container was empty.

In the ensuing darkness, Caitlin groped for the light switch. The dusky illumination of the overhead light barely pierced the smoky gloom. She heard Linnie cough behind her, and then begin to struggle with the window

105

latch. Sweet night air swept into the room, and the smoke began to dissipate.

Jeff leaned against the wall, coughing, the empty extinguisher dangling from one hand. Caitlin caught him in a fierce embrace.

"You foolish, foolish child!" she exclaimed. "You could have been killed!" Her tears soaked his shoulder as she wept and hugged him close, terrified by the idea that she might have lost him.

Linnie stood limply, surveying the mess of charred wood and chemical foam. "What happened?" she cried.

"Let's get out of here first," Caitlin said as she pushed the two, choking and coughing, ahead of her into the night. They stood together, arms around each other, breathing the clean, cool air and coughing out remnants of smoke.

"Now, Jeff. Explain," Caitlin said when she'd caught her breath.

Jeff coughed again and spit in the dirt before replying. "I came down to get a drink and happened to glance out the kitchen window. I saw the fire and yelled for you. Then I came to put it out."

"Oh, Jeff!" Caitlin hugged him hard. "What if something had happened to you?"

"But it didn't." Jeff sounded more like his old self every minute. "And I couldn't just stand there and watch all we've slaved for go up in smoke, could I?"

"We owe Spring Hollow to you, in more ways than one," Caitlin said gratefully. "Now let's call the fire department."

"What for?" Linnie asked. "The fire's out."

"True," Caitlin said as they made their way back to the house, "but it started somehow, and I want to know how. And we'll have to have everything inspected again. Thank goodness we installed the fire extinguisher.''

The first faint light of dawn nudged the mountains as Caitlin hung up the phone. ''The fire truck's on the way, and the fire marshal will be out later to investigate,'' she said. ''I think that, under the circumstances, we'll skip church today. I'll stay up and wait for the firemen. You two go on back to bed.''

Linnie's head rested on the kitchen table, and Jeff stretched and yawned. ''I could use some more sleep. What do you want me to do with these pajamas?'' he asked.

Caitlin shuddered as she looked at the soot-stained, flame-scorched nightclothes. ''Throw them out. I never want to see them again.''

She and Jeff helped Linnie upstairs and into bed. Jeff stripped off his pajamas and drew on a pair of sweatpants, then collapsed across his bed and fell asleep immediately.

Caitlin shed her smoky nightgown, shivering in the chill of dawn, and wrapped herself tightly in a woolen robe. She brushed her teeth and then stepped into the shower, letting the steaming water wash away the last of the smoke and grime, enjoying the slide of hot water over her skin.

She toweled herself dry and fluffed her damp brown hair into place with her fingers. She chose a bright, spring green jumpsuit to wear, feeling the need for something pretty after the dark horror of the early morning hours. Dawn spread its fingers of rose and apricot across the eastern horizon, and shafts of sparkling golden light heralded the rising sun. The black memory of the hours just past faded in the growing light of morning.

She puttered in the kitchen, snacking on toast, not

wanting to fix breakfast, not really hungry. The sun rose higher, hot in a clear blue sky, the storm of yesterday only a memory in the puddles in the driveway.

The fire truck pulled into the yard, and Caitlin led the way to the guesthouse. She stood back, reluctant to enter. The crew chief pushed the door open, and he and his mates entered the barn. Caitlin inched to the doorway and peered in. The part of the room she could see from the doorway discouraged her, and she sighed and shook her head in defeat.

The crew chief came out. "It's not too bad," he said, and the kindness in his voice made Caitlin want to weep.

"What started it?" she asked.

"That's for the fire marshal to determine," he said, "but there's very little damage. Mostly smoke and chemicals from the extinguisher. I don't think it'll take too long to clean it up."

"Thanks," Caitlin replied. "I appreciate your coming out."

"No problem," he said as they walked back toward the fire truck. "The fire marshal will be out later."

Caitlin watched them pull out, then went back to her toast and tea.

Around ten, Linnie wandered into the kitchen, yawning and poking into the refrigerator for something to eat. Jeff slumbered on.

"Do you want me to fix you some breakfast?" Caitlin asked.

"No, thanks. I'm not too hungry," Linnie said as she spooned up some of the leftover dessert that Mae had brought to the party. "I think I'll go shower."

She went upstairs, and soon Caitlin heard the water running. Over the sound of the shower, she heard a vehicle pull up in the ranch yard. The fire marshal had arrived.

"Good morning. Miss Morrisey? I'm Inspector Nelson. You had a fire?" He eyed the house, and Caitlin pointed to the barn.

"Yes. My brother got up to get a drink of water about three this morning and noticed flames in our guesthouse," she explained as she led the way across the parking area. "Fortunately we had a fire extinguisher handy, and Jeff put the fire out before the whole place went up."

"You haven't moved anything? Touched anything?" he asked.

"I thought I'd better wait until you got here," Caitlin replied.

"Good." Inspector Nelson stepped into the barn and looked around. Caitlin followed. In the full light of late morning, the charred spot on the wall didn't look as bad as it had in the smoky nightmare of dawn.

Nelson prodded at something with his pen. "Have you been painting?" he asked.

"Yes. You see, we're just opening this up as a guest ranch, and our official opening was yesterday," Caitlin said. "We got all the furniture moved in and . . ." Her voice trailed away as she fought tears. How long, she wondered, would it take to repair the damage?

"Well, it looks like someone was a little careless with the paint rags. They shouldn't have been left lying around. Spontaneous combustion's what started your fire."

"What?" Caitlin whispered. "That's not possible. All the painting supplies were taken away by the contractor. We don't have any paint or rags in here."

"Take a look for yourself," he said. "These rags were

piled here in the corner, and must have ignited spontaneously.''

Caitlin leaned closer. ''Inspector, those were not here yesterday afternoon. Someone brought them in and set them on fire.''

''You're sure?''

''I'm positive they weren't here,'' she said. ''You can ask anyone who was here yesterday. Someone would have noticed them. The smell alone would have alerted us. No, we wouldn't have a housewarming with paint rags lying around.'' Her voice was scornful.

''Then someone started the fire, hoping that the whole building would burn and cover up the evidence,'' he said, frowning. ''I'll call the sheriff's office. May I use your phone?''

''Certainly.'' She led the way back to the house and gave him the phone in the living room.

Jeff was up and around, and Caitlin explained to him and Linnie what Inspector Nelson had found.

''Someone's trying to put us out of business before we even get started,'' she said.

''Do you suppose this has anything to do with our trespasser?'' Linnie asked.

''I don't know, but I'm certainly going to mention it to the deputy,'' Caitlin said. ''But why on earth would anyone want us to fail?''

Jeff shrugged, and Linnie looked as puzzled as Caitlin felt.

''Someone will be out shortly to investigate,'' Inspector Nelson said as he entered the kitchen. ''Arson is a very serious matter. I hope we can find the perpetrator.''

''How soon can we start cleaning up?'' Caitlin asked. ''We have brochures distributed around town. We could start getting reservations anytime.''

"We'll be done this afternoon," he said. "Then you can clean up. It doesn't look like there's much structural damage—a couple of boards need to be replaced, but you were lucky."

"Thank goodness for thirsty brothers," Linnie said fervently.

"You must be the young man who put out the fire," Nelson said as he shook Jeff's hand. "That was quick thinking."

Jeff blushed and said, "I just remembered where the fire extinguisher was. It's a good thing the insurance company made us put one in."

"Oh, here's the sheriff now," Caitlin said. "And Connor!"

Inspector Nelson went out, and he and the deputy walked over to the barn. Connor Devlin watched them for a moment, then took the porch stairs two at a time.

Caitlin opened the door before he could knock.

"Cait, what's going on?" His strong hands on her shoulders made Caitlin's knees tremble. She sat down at the table in self-defense.

"Someone tried to burn down the barn last night," she said. "If Jeff hadn't gotten up for a drink of water, the whole thing would have burned to the ground."

Connor's lips thinned and his steely eyes narrowed. "I'd like to find the guy who started it. He wouldn't be a problem ever again. How bad is it?"

She shrugged at his question. "The inspector doesn't think it's too bad," she replied. "Mostly we'll have to air the place out and wash all the linens. And just when I had everything clean!" She sighed in exasperation. "We might have to replace a couple of boards, too."

"When can we start?" Connor asked.

''Sometime this afternoon, I think,'' she said, ''but you don't have to—''

''I want to. That's what friends are for. And we are friends, aren't we?'' A slight smile tugged at his mouth, and Caitlin noticed that his eyes now mirrored the sky. She forced herself to look away and tried to ignore the way her pulse raced when he was near.

''Thanks. I think I'd rather have you for a friend than for an enemy,'' she said with sincerity.

Later, Inspector Nelson and the deputy stood near the sheriff's car, and Caitlin and Connor and the kids went out to hear what they had to say.

''You can go in now,'' Inspector Nelson said. ''We have all the evidence we need. I'll let you know what the lab finds.''

''Thank you,'' Caitlin said. ''Okay, kids, it's laundry time.''

Linnie groaned and went into the house to get the laundry basket. Jeff and Connor walked toward the guesthouse, discussing the best way to air the mattresses.

Caitlin caught up with them at the door. Now that the smoke had cleared, the bright light of day showed minimal damage to the room. Connor examined the scorched wall and floorboards. ''It's not too bad,'' he said. ''You have some scrap lumber left over, don't you?''

''Yeah. It's over in the new barn,'' Jeff said. ''Dad's tools are in there, too.''

There was an uncomfortable moment of silence as they remembered the accident and its probable cause. Connor tensed, ready for more accusations from Caitlin. Jeff looked at them, not sure what to expect.

''Well, are you just going to stand there all day?'' she asked, her voice shaky. ''We have a business to salvage.'' She smiled at Connor, and his face relaxed into what, for him, passed as a smile.

"Come on, Jeff," he said. "Let's see what we can find."

They spent the afternoon airing, cleaning, washing, and repairing. Connor cut out the burned wood and replaced it with new boards. By dark, the only evidence that there had been a fire was a slight, lingering scent of smoke.

"Leave the windows open all night and you won't even notice it by morning," Connor advised.

"Would you like to stay for supper?" Caitlin asked. "It's the least I can offer."

"Maybe some other time," he said. "I have some things to take care of at home." His voice was casual, but his eyes spoke his regret at having to turn down her invitation.

"Well, thanks again for all your help," she said, holding out her hand to shake his.

He took both of her hands in his, and an electric spark tingled up her arms. Why did his touch move her so much? His lips caressed her cheek briefly; then he released her hands, saluted her with his fingertips, and turned to go.

She touched her cheek gently, feeling the burning of his lips as if they still lingered there. Then, shaking herself, she went into the house, hoping the coming days wouldn't be as eventful as the opening day of business had been.

Chapter Twelve

Caitlin smoothed the spread over the newly made bed in the suite of the guesthouse. Connor's advice had been sound. After a night of fresh air, there was nothing left of the scorched smell. The mattresses were aired, and the sheets, dried outdoors in the sunshine, brought the scent of summer into the barn. Jeff had helped her move the beds back into place before he and Linnie had left for school. Once more they were ready for business.

She stretched and rubbed the small of her back, then went downstairs. Out in the yard, she pinched off a few wilting petunia blossoms as she crossed to the house. As she glanced back toward the guesthouse, the old barn windows sparkled in the morning light, and the new curtains ruffled in the breeze. The flower beds were carpets of color against the old rail fence, and the picnic area, with its barbecue pit and rustic tables, invited guests to relax in the shade of the giant cottonwood that hung over it.

The telephone's shrill ring startled her from her reverie. She bounded up the porch steps two at a time and grabbed the receiver.

"Hello?" she said breathlessly.

"Is this the Spring Hollow Guest Ranch?" a man's voice inquired.

"Yes, it is," Caitlin replied calmly, although she felt as if she would choke on her excitement.

"My family and I would like to stay for a week, starting today. Do you have room?"

"Certainly, sir. How many in your family?" Caitlin jotted notes on a pad near the phone.

"My wife and myself, and our two sons."

"We have a two-bedroom suite available," she explained. "One room has two twin beds, and the other has a double bed. Will that be satisfactory?"

"That sounds fine," he replied. "The name is Gray. Mr. and Mrs. William Gray. We're in Montrose now, so how long will it take us to drive out?"

"About an hour," she said, holding her excitement in check, trying to act as though she took reservations every day of the week. "Do you have one of our brochures?"

"Yes. We picked it up at the chamber of commerce."

"There's a map on the back. Just take the highway east out of town and watch for the turn. I'll see you in about an hour."

Caitlin hung up and jumped around the kitchen, screaming like a kid on a carnival ride. "Our very first guests!" she shouted to no one.

She ran outside and picked a huge bouquet of fresh flowers and brought them into the kitchen to arrange them. As she tucked sweet-scented phlox in among the taller larkspur, she sang to herself. The first of the roses mingled nicely with the blue and purple of the other flowers.

She carried the vase over to the guesthouse and put it on the dining table, arranging a stem here and a blossom there. She quickly toured the remodeled barn to make sure that everything was spotless.

Back in the house, she took three chickens from the

refrigerator and put a pot of beans on to soak. "Let's see," she mused, "seven to feed . . . three should be enough. And I'll have time to make biscuits. Then a salad."

She worked quickly, cutting the chicken into pieces, preparing a butter-herb basting sauce, chopping vegetables for a salad. As she worked, she planned breakfast. She'd get up early and make some apple muffins. There was plenty of milk, and scrambled eggs would go well with the muffins and coffee.

Just as she reached for the cookbook to find her favorite cherry cake recipe, the Grays arrived.

Caitlin hoped her nervousness didn't show as she went out to greet them. Her legs shook, and she wiped damp palms on her jeans. Would she like them? Would they like her? Would they have a good time? The questions spun in her head like windmills in a hurricane.

Mr. Gray went around the car to open his wife's door while the two boys piled out of the backseat. Mrs. Gray stretched and smiled at Caitlin.

"Hello," she said. "We're the Grays."

"I'm Caitlin Morrisey, but you can call me Cait."

Mr. Gray shook hands and said, "I'm Bill, and this is Rita. Boys, this is Cait. Cait, this is Terry, and the younger one is Mike."

"How do you do?" the boys replied in unison. Terry seemed to be about twelve, and Mike about nine.

"The guesthouse is over there." Caitlin pointed. "You can park in front. It'll be easier to unload your luggage."

She and Mrs. Gray and the boys walked across the barnyard as Mr. Gray swung the car up next to the fence that surrounded the old barn.

"What a lovely place!" Mrs. Gray exclaimed. "You must love living here."

"Oh, we do," Caitlin replied. "It's been in the family for generations, and I couldn't imagine growing up anywhere else."

Mrs. Gray nodded. "I've always been a city girl, and the boys, too. We're from Denver. We've been looking for a place to really get back to nature, a place where we don't have to dress up or *do* things all the time. Last year we went to a dude ranch in Arizona, and it was almost like being in the army. They planned our vacation so minutely that we didn't have time to enjoy ourselves."

"Well, you certainly won't have that problem here," Caitlin said with a laugh. "You're free to come and go as you wish." She smiled at the boys. "There's plenty of room to explore. The only place that's off-limits is the new barn. We have livestock in there, and I'd rather you didn't play around them. But as soon as Jeff and Linnie— my brother and sister—get home from school, I'd bet that Jeff will saddle up the horses for you."

"Horses! Oh, boy!" Terry shouted. Mike echoed his excitement.

Mr. Gray called, "Come give me a hand with the suitcases." Terry and Mike hurried to help their father.

Caitlin led the way into the guesthouse, then stood aside as Mr. and Mrs. Gray and the boys entered.

"What a lovely room," Mrs. Gray said. "It's so comfortable and homey."

"I hope you'll enjoy staying with us," Caitlin said. "Your rooms are upstairs." Mike and Terry lugged their suitcases up the wooden steps, and their parents followed. Caitlin brought up the rear.

"The two rooms share a bath," she pointed out. "There's a stove and refrigerator downstairs if you want to fix lunch or snacks. Breakfast and dinner are included in the price of the rooms."

"Great," Mr. Gray said. "Boys, can you get the cooler out of the trunk? We'll get our picnic stuff put away."

Terry and Mike raced downstairs, and the grown-ups followed more slowly.

Mr. Gray pulled out his wallet. "Let me pay you for five days," he said.

"Thank you," Caitlin said as he counted bills into her hand. "I'll get you a receipt and the keys for your rooms. The main door isn't ever locked, but each guest room has its own key. But since you're the only ones here, you probably won't have to bother locking up."

"I'm sure we'll be fine," Mrs. Gray said.

"Good. Dinner's at six-thirty. We'll grill some chicken outdoors and eat under the trees. In the meantime, relax and enjoy yourselves." Caitlin turned and waved as she walked back to the house.

Once inside, she recounted the roll of bills he'd given her. There was enough to pay for Linnie's graduation dress and take the kids out for lunch after the ceremony.

"I can't believe Linnie will be out of school in less than a week," she said to herself. She sighed and dabbed at her eyes as she thought of her parents and how they would have enjoyed the preparations for graduation. But the time for regrets was past. Only the future mattered now.

Jeff burst into the kitchen. "Whose car?" he asked. Linnie followed him a little more sedately, but echoed his question.

"Do we have guests?" she asked.

"Yes, we do. A family named Gray. They have two boys, and Jeff, I practically promised them that you'd saddle up Rough and Ready when you got home."

"My first trail ride!" he exclaimed.

"They're a little young. You might try them out in the corral first, just to see how they ride."

Jeff reached for a piece of cake, and Caitlin swatted his hand away. "For dinner. Have a banana," she said.

"You know, Cait, we're going to need a couple more horses," Jeff said as he peeled the fruit. "If we have more than one person who wants to ride, I can't go along."

"I know." Caitlin pondered a moment. "We can't afford to buy more horses right now. Where could we find some to board?"

Linnie spoke up. "Jessica's folks have three horses that have done nothing but eat their heads off since the boys went away to college. Jessica hardly ever rides anymore. I wonder if they'd let us use them in exchange for taking care of them?"

"What a great idea! Can you call now?" Caitlin asked.

"Sure." Linnie dialed the number and tapped her foot impatiently while she waited for an answer.

Caitlin and Jeff walked out to the new barn and called Rough and Ready in from the pasture. Mike and Terry Gray hovered near the guesthouse, anxious to ride but not wanting to get in the way, until Jeff waved and shouted, "Come on over. I need someone to help exercise these guys."

The boys raced across the ranch yard, climbed up on the corral fence, and watched eagerly as Caitlin and Jeff saddled the two chestnut horses. Jeff led Rough over to the fence, and Terry slipped into the saddle as Caitlin edged Ready up next to Mike. The younger boy hesitated a moment, then plunked into the saddle and grabbed the saddle horn.

"Have you guys ridden before?" Jeff asked.

"Just a couple of times," Terry said.

"Okay. Tell you what. We'll stay in the corral for now and you can practice." Caitlin left Jeff explaining the finer points of guiding a horse and went back to the house.

"It's all set," Linnie said. "Jessica's folks thought it was a wonderful idea. Mr. Walsh will bring them over tomorrow."

"Super! That means getting some more stalls ready. Can you take care of that while I start the fire in the barbecue?"

"Sure. Just let me get changed." Linnie dashed upstairs.

Caitlin made several trips from the woodpile to the stone fireplace under the cottonwoods, stockpiling enough logs to keep the fire going well. She knelt and built a small teepee of twigs and kindling, and touched a match to it. As the flames grew, she added larger pieces until the fire burned hot and high. The scrub oak smelled like autumn leaves burning and would leave a perfect bed of coals for cooking.

The beans simmered on the stove, and Caitlin sniffed appreciatively as she mixed the biscuit dough. She liked to cook, and she wanted this dinner to be perfect. The reputation of the Spring Hollow Guest Ranch was resting on what the Grays thought of their hospitality.

Linnie came in, brushing straw from her jeans, and washed her hands at the kitchen sink. "Everything's ready," she said.

"Thanks, kid. Now, what about graduation? When do you have to be in town Saturday?"

Linnie sat down and watched Caitlin roll out the dough and cut it into neat circles with a drinking glass turned upside down. "The ceremony starts at ten, and they told us to be there by nine at the latest."

"Okay. We'll be on the road by eight. Did you get your cap and gown yet?"

"Not until Friday," Linnie replied. "Mr. James will hand them out in the morning."

Caitlin smiled at her sister. "Are you excited?"

Linnie twisted her class ring around and around on her finger. "Kind of, but I'm scared, too, you know? It's like the end of my life, or the beginning. I don't know which. Sometimes I wish I could just go on and on, going to classes, not having to think about college or getting a job or anything."

"I know what you mean." Caitlin shook her head ruefully. "It's a pretty changeable time. Unfortunately, college is out of the question this year. We just can't afford it."

"I know. I'm not sure that's what I want anyway. I think I'd be better off working somewhere for a while."

"Well, you'll certainly be working around here this summer if we get busy," Caitlin said. "Once we get organized, I'd like to start saving part of what we make for you and Jeff, either for college later on, or whatever you want to use it for. But right now, I'm depending on you guys to help me make Spring Hollow a success."

Linnie went to the refrigerator and poured a glass of milk. "We're in this together, Cait. Jeff and I will do our parts. You can count on us," she said, her voice serious as she turned to face her sister.

"I know, and I appreciate it," Caitlin replied. "Here, slide these in the oven while I put the chicken on the fire." She handed Linnie the tray of biscuits and hoisted the roasting pan full of chicken pieces.

Mr. and Mrs. Gray sat at the picnic table, savoring the golden light of early evening. A slight breeze set the cottonwood leaves twinkling and rustling. Mr. Gray rose and took the pan of chicken from Caitlin.

"Here. I'll put that on for you," he said. "I'm known as the king of the barbecue at home." He struck a mock pose of royalty, and his wife laughed and faked a kick at his rear.

Caitlin handed the pan over with a smile. "Thanks. I didn't expect you to do the chores. I'll run back and get the basting sauce." She quickly returned, and soon the pungent smoke of the cooking meat rose in the evening air, signaling Jeff and the boys that it was time to stable the horses and clean up.

The Grays gathered at the picnic table, and Jeff and Linnie carried out the rest of the food.

"You can all start with salad," Caitlin said, as she turned and basted the chicken once again. "This will be ready by the time you finish."

Terry reached for the salad. "This is great. I love to eat outside."

"Me too," Mike piped up.

"You just love to eat," Terry teased.

"Do not!" Mike protested, frowning as he helped himself to salad.

"Boys." Mrs. Gray's voice was firm, and the squabble subsided.

Caitlin, her face flushed from the heat of the fire, set the platter of chicken in front of Mrs. Gray. "Why don't you start? We'll just pass everything around."

Conversation slackened as they occupied themselves with the food. Soon only empty dishes and a pile of chicken bones remained.

"This mountain air sure gives me an appetite," Mr. Gray said.

"Yes, and it's cooling off quickly," his wife added.

"Terry, run and get me my pink sweater, please. It's on the chair in the bedroom."

"Okay, Mom." Terry ran off with Mike right behind him.

Caitlin stacked the dishes, and Linnie carried them to the house. She returned with dessert plates and the cake.

Mr. Gray held up a hand. "This is too tempting." He groaned. "If I'd known you had this around, I wouldn't have had that last piece of chicken. But I think I have room for just a tiny piece."

"Here you are, Mom. Oh, boy! Cake!" Terry said.

The boys sat down and eagerly accepted the pieces that Linnie handed them.

"You know, this is kind of like camp," Terry said, "with the fire and everything. We told ghost stories last year, every night. Do you know any ghost stories?" he asked Jeff.

"Oh, you don't want spooky stories just before bed," his mother protested.

"Sure we do, Mom," Mike said. "We don't get scared, just interested."

Jeff leaned closer to the boys. "I don't know any ghost stories, but I've got a great story about buried treasure. Okay?" He looked questioningly at Mrs. Gray.

"All right," she conceded, "if it's a short one."

Jeff rested his elbows on the table and lowered his voice conspiratorially. "Well, the story starts a couple of hundred years ago, long before Colorado was a state, and before many white men had ever set foot in the mountains. The Spanish came up from Mexico and explored most of the southwest part of the country. They even came all the way up here, right on this ranch." His voice dropped dramatically, and Mike's fork paused in midair.

"Then what?" Terry prodded.

"Well, this one group of explorers found a vein of almost pure gold running through a quartz outcropping. They hacked out as much of it as they could and melted it down into bars. Their packhorses could hardly walk, they were so loaded with gold.

"By this time, it was late in the year and the snow had started. The Spaniards weren't prepared to spend the winter in the mountains, but they couldn't travel fast because of the gold.

"So they found a cave and hid the treasure, vowing to come back in the spring. They rolled some rocks over the entrance and made a map on a piece of leather.

"They rode away, back south toward Mexico. Unfortunately, they were attacked by a band of Indians, Apaches, and massacred, all but one. He survived and managed to crawl to the nearest settlement, with the map tucked inside his shirt."

Jeff's gaze swept the audience. No one moved.

"He was crippled for life by the Indian attack and never came back for the treasure. He gave the map to his son and swore him to secrecy. The next spring the son set out for the mountains.

"The father waited and waited for his son to return, but the young man vanished. No one ever saw the map or the treasure again."

"Wow!" Mike said. "Is that a true story?"

Jeff grinned. "There are lots of people who have believed it and searched for the treasure. As far as I know, it's still out there somewhere."

"Wouldn't it be neat if we could find it?" Terry exclaimed. "Boy, we'd be rich!"

"If it's been lost for two hundred years, I doubt you'll find it in the next few days," Mrs. Gray said, "but it makes a good story."

''I hate to put an end to this,'' Mr. Gray said as he stood and put a hand on Mike's shoulder, ''but it's been a long day. You'll have to hunt for treasure tomorrow.''

''I've still got some math to finish,'' Jeff said as he stretched and yawned.

''And I've got to finish that history chapter,'' Linnie said. ''Good night.''

The Grays said their good nights, and soon Caitlin sat alone, watching the embers die. The night closed in around her, dark sapphire sprinkled with stars, cool and serene. She thought about the day just past. If all their guests turned out to be as pleasant as the Grays, the guest ranch would be an overwhelming success.

The coals cooled from red to tarnished pewter, and she sighed and rose. As she walked toward the house, wrapped in a glow of happiness, she glanced toward the north pasture. Just for an instant, a light glowed small and lost against the bulk of Storm King Mountain.

Caitlin stared hard into the darkness, searching for another flash of light, but only the shadowed night remained. Maybe she was seeing things. She'd only glimpsed it out of the corner of her eye. She rubbed her eyes and looked again. No lights anywhere in the north pasture or on the mountain that loomed over it.

''It's just my imagination,'' she said as she hurried up the porch steps. But sleep was long in coming.

Chapter Thirteen

The high school gym was already hot at nine-thirty in the morning. The sound of rustling programs filled the air as people fanned themselves, and a low murmur of conversation permeated the room as they waited for the ceremony to begin. Linnie had disappeared into the lunchroom, where the graduates were putting on their caps and gowns, and lining up in alphabetical order. Caitlin and Jeff sat near the front of the room, where flowers in the school colors flanked the stage. They could hear the school band tuning up in the lobby.

At exactly ten o'clock, the band struck up ''Pomp and Circumstance,'' and the superintendent and the principal led the procession into the gym. Caitlin craned her neck to see Linnie come in, and Jeff readied his camera.

Linnie marched slowly and calmly down the aisle, and Jeff stood to snap her picture. She smiled at them as she passed. Caitlin's heart beat faster as she remembered her own high school graduation.

Would she ever graduate from college? Quickly she dismissed the thought. Finishing college was in the future, and there was no point in thinking about it now. She concentrated on the ceremony.

The graduation speaker droned on and on, as Caitlin perspired and wished he'd finish. Finally he sat down to heartfelt applause, and she wondered if he knew it was because he was finished and not because his speech was particularly inspiring.

The valedictorian gave her address, fortunately a short one, and then the black-gowned seniors advanced, one by one, to claim their diplomas. Jeff snapped several pictures as Linnie ascended the steps to the stage and shook hands with the principal. Caitlin saw tears in her sister's eyes as she stepped down from the stage and returned to her seat, but Linnie managed to smile for Jeff as he took one last picture.

The last graduate left the stage, and the superintendent declared graduation over. Once again the band played and the graduates marched out, followed by the audience.

The Morriseys gathered on the lawn, and Jeff took more pictures in the clear May light. Caitlin snapped one of Linnie and Jeff together; then Linnie pulled off her robe with a sigh of relief.

"Whew! These things are heavy," she said as she wiped perspiration from her brow. "I'll return this and be right back."

"Okay. We'll meet you at the truck," Caitlin said.

The restaurant was crowded, and they had to wait for several minutes before a table opened up. Most of the graduates and their relatives and friends had come for lunch, and people visited back and forth between tables.

"Order anything you want," Caitlin advised her siblings as the waiter handed them leather-bound menus. "Price is no object. We're celebrating."

"Steak for me," Linnie said, "and a baked potato with lots of butter and sour cream."

"I'll have the breaded pork chops with mashed potatoes and gravy," Jeff decided.

Caitlin ordered chicken cordon bleu with a baked potato.

"Just help yourselves to the salad bar whenever you're ready," the waiter said.

"How does it feel to be out of school?" Caitlin asked Linnie as they returned to the table with salad plates heaped high.

"Great!" she replied. "But I thought that guy was never going to stop talking. He said that today is the first day of the rest of our lives, but I thought that I was going to have to wait until tomorrow to start living—he sounded like he was going to talk all night."

Caitlin laughed. "It was the same at my graduation."

Jeff shook his head in disgust. "If I have to sit through a speech that boring when I graduate, I think I'll just ask them to mail my diploma. Or I could drop out." He looked hopefully at Caitlin.

"No way, José," she countered. "You're in for the duration. Besides, now there are only three years left to go."

Jeff made a face and attacked his salad with a vengeance.

Caitlin speared a lettuce leaf and raised it to her mouth. She stopped, fork in midair, as she recognized a dark head across the room. Connor Devlin had just entered the restaurant. He stood waiting for the hostess to seat him, but every table in the dining room was full. His jeans fit his muscular legs tightly, and his shirt stretched across his broad torso. Caitlin's stomach fluttered as he looked straight into her eyes. Then he looked away. Her heart dropped just as Linnie saw him, too.

Linnie waved encouragingly and stopped the waiter. "Would you tell Mr. Devlin that there's an extra seat here?" she asked.

"Sure." There was no need for him to ask who Connor was; everyone knew everyone else in the small community. He wound his way through the tables, holding his tray high above his head, and Caitlin saw him talk and point to their table.

"I don't think you should have done that, Linnie," she said. "He might not want to share a table."

"Oh, fiddle. Here he comes," her sister said. "I wonder why we haven't seen him since the fire?"

Connor towered over them, his face grim at first, but lightening into a slight smile as he looked at Linnie. "Congratulations," he said. "How does it feel to be out of school?"

"Great!" Linnie said. "Why don't you sit with us and help us celebrate?"

"Sure," Jeff chimed in.

Connor glanced at Caitlin, and she nodded to the empty chair next to her. As he slid into the seat, she noticed that his eyes were steely gray. *What's his problem?* she wondered as the waiter took his order.

Jeff and Linnie seemed oblivious to Caitlin's discomfort and Connor's mood. They chattered like jaybirds, giving him an extensive report on the happenings at Spring Hollow. Caitlin ate silently, very much aware of Connor's nearness in the crowded restaurant, yet reluctant to move away from him. So far he hadn't said a word to her.

"So where have you been the last several days or so?" Jeff finally asked. "We thought you'd be over to see how we're doing."

Connor cleared his throat. "I had to go to Denver to take care of some business," he said. "I just got back the day before yesterday."

"Well, we're glad to see you," Linnie said.

His face softened as he smiled at the graduate. ''I'm glad to see you, too.''

Caitlin noticed that he didn't look at her when he said it.

''Cait, tell him about the Grays,'' Jeff urged. ''They're our first customers,'' he explained to Connor.

''Oh, you go ahead,'' she replied. ''You spent more time with them than I did.''

''Yeah, it was really great,'' Jeff continued. ''The kids wanted to ride all the time, and their parents were real nice. I hope all our guests are as nice.''

Connor leaned to his right as the waiter set his dinner in front of him, and his shoulder brushed Caitlin's. Even that slight touch sent tingles up her arm. She wanted to lean against him and let him hold her forever, but she drew away slightly and cut the last piece of her chicken.

Connor concentrated on his meal, content to let the two younger people carry the conversation. Occasionally he glanced at Caitlin as if puzzled about something.

The Morriseys had finished eating. Caitlin folded her napkin and laid it on the table. ''Well, kids, are you ready to head home?'' she asked.

''I guess so,'' Linnie replied. ''I don't think I'll feel really graduated until I get home and don't have to come back to school.'' She smiled at Connor. ''Did you have the same feeling when you graduated?''

''Yes. Both times,'' he said.

''Both?'' Caitlin questioned.

''Yes. High school and college.''

''I didn't know you went to college,'' Jeff said.

Connor finished swallowing and said, ''I graduated from Colorado State University in Fort Collins. I majored in agriculture and business.''

Caitlin raised her eyebrows. "I had no idea you were so talented," she said.

"Not much talent involved," he said as he wiped his mouth. "Just a lot of hard work and a sense of purpose. Kind of like you." He looked at her directly for the first time.

"What do you mean?" she asked.

"What you've done with the ranch," he replied. "I really didn't think you'd get it off the ground, but you surprised me."

She shrugged and looked away. "I just had to do something, and this seemed to be the best idea we could come up with, other than finding that old Spanish treasure." She chuckled. "And I don't think there's much chance of that." She pushed back her chair and reached for her purse.

Connor rose, too. "I'd like to come over and talk to you tonight," he said. "If that's convenient."

"Of course." She glanced at him curiously. "You're welcome anytime. You know that."

For just a moment, his eyes sparked blue; then they faded back to gray. "I'll see you about eight," he said.

"I'll look forward to it," she replied.

They drove back to the ranch in high spirits, Jeff and Linnie because of graduation, Caitlin because she'd be seeing Connor in a few short hours.

They pulled into the ranch yard just in time to greet two couples who had seen their brochure and had come out to spend the night.

"I hope you have room," one of the women said. "We tried to call from town but didn't get an answer."

Caitlin apologized. "My sister just graduated from high school this morning, and we stopped for a celebration lunch."

''Well, congratulations!'' the woman's husband exclaimed, shaking Linnie's hand.

''We're the Norrises,'' the woman said, ''and these are our friends, the Wests.''

''We're glad to have you,'' Caitlin said. ''Jeff, why don't you take them over to the guesthouse while I change? I'll only be a minute,'' she said to the couples.

She hurried upstairs and changed into a pair of jeans and a coral blouse and tossed her dress into the hamper. She paused at the mirror to run a comb through her dark hair, then hurried down the stairs two at a time and ran across the yard to the guesthouse.

The Norrises and Wests had settled into the two lower rooms and were exploring the common room. Jeff was busy carrying in suitcases.

''No television?'' Mrs. West asked.

''No,'' Caitlin said. ''We're too far out for cable, and we can't get any of the local channels—too many mountains in the way.''

''Never mind, Karen,'' her husband said. ''We came out here for peace and quiet. You can last one night without watching the news.''

''I suppose so,'' Karen West muttered.

Caitlin cringed inside. She didn't want to deal with a dissatisfied guest, especially when there was nothing she could do to fix the problem.

''Well,'' she said brightly, ''we have lots of other things to do. If you ride, we have a stable. No extra charge,'' she added quickly as she caught sight of Mrs. West's expression.

''And we'll have dinner around six. Since the weather's so nice, we can cook the steaks outside and eat at the picnic table. And I can bring breakfast over whenever you're ready for it.''

"Sounds great," Mr. Norris said. "We haven't had a cookout in ages."

Mrs. West looked as if she was going to say something unpleasant, but her husband's hand on her arm kept her silent.

"I'll see you later, then," Caitlin said as she followed Jeff out the door.

As soon as they were out of hearing distance, Jeff said, "Wow! What's her problem?"

"I don't know, but I'm glad they're staying just one night. Can you imagine a week of putting up with her?"

"No way!"

Dinner came and went without more unpleasantness from Mrs. West, but Caitlin was on tenterhooks, waiting for more criticism. Jeff and Linnie ate in the house.

The other three more than made up for Mrs. West's bad attitude. They loved everything about Spring Hollow and assured Caitlin that they would tell their friends about it.

"Any chance of an early morning ride?" Mr. Norris asked.

"Sure. How early do you want to start?" Caitlin asked.

"Oh, how does seven-thirty sound?" he asked, looking at the others.

"That sounds good to me," Mrs. Norris said, and Mr. West agreed.

"You know I always sleep in on Sunday," Mrs. West snapped.

Mr. West scowled but said, "Looks like we'll only need three horses, then."

"Jeff will have them ready by seven-thirty," Caitlin

said hastily. ''Would you like breakfast before or after your ride?''

''Oh, after, definitely,'' Mrs. Norris said. ''I couldn't bump around on a horse after eating.'' She laughed and added, ''Just a cup of coffee first thing.''

''There's an automatic-drip coffeemaker on the counter, and coffee and filters in the cupboard,'' Caitlin said. ''Please help yourselves.''

''You mean we have to make our own coffee? I thought *you* provided breakfast.'' Mrs. West's tone was that of a queen talking to a kitchen slave.

Caitlin flushed, but kept her voice even as she replied, ''I can certainly come over and start the coffee about seven if it won't disturb you.''

Mr. Norris broke in. ''Don't bother. I think I can manage to brew a pot of coffee.'' He gave Karen West a disgusted look.

Mrs. West folded her arms and looked up at the cottonwood leaves dancing in the evening breeze, ignoring the reprimand.

''I'll plan on breakfast when you come back, then,'' Caitlin said. She turned to Mrs. West. ''Of course, if you'd like yours before they come back, just let me know. Now I'll say good night.''

She made her escape, burdened with the dirty dishes from supper, thankful to have them as an excuse to get away from that awful woman.

As she crossed the yard, Connor pulled up. ''I'll take these,'' he said as he relieved her of the dirty dishes.

''Thanks,'' she replied. ''We just finished supper. Boy, it was a long one!'' She sighed.

''Bad people?'' he asked as he set the dishes on the counter.

''Not really,'' Caitlin said, ''but Mrs. West is determined to find fault with everything I do. If I weren't so well brought up, I'd hang a name on her.'' She turned the faucet handle vigorously, then jumped as the spray of water drenched her blouse. Connor grabbed the dish towel for her.

Just at that moment, brown eyes stared into blue. . . . Connor's lips came down to cover hers, and she closed her eyes and clung to him. His arms encircled her, pulling her against his chest.

Footsteps clattered down the hall, and they sprang apart. Caitlin blushed furiously as she turned to face Jeff.

He didn't seem to notice their discomfiture. ''Hey, Cait, what's on for tomorrow?''

Caitlin pulled her soaked blouse away from her skin. ''Early morning ride,'' she said, trying to maintain an air of innocence. ''Just let me go change and I'll tell you all about it.'' She hurried from the room, afraid that her brother could read her thoughts.

By the time she'd changed her shirt and come back downstairs, Jeff and Connor had the dishes washed, dried, and put away. *Calm down now,* she admonished herself. *One kiss does not a relationship make.*

''So what time do I have to be ready?'' Jeff asked as he hung the dish towel up.

''They want to ride out about seven-thirty,'' Caitlin said. ''I'll get you up about an hour before that.''

''Sounds good,'' he said. ''I'd better go get ready for bed if I have to ride herd on those tenderfeet in the morning. See you.'' He shook hands with Connor and left.

Caitlin's awkwardness fled as Connor said, ''Sit down. I want to talk to you.'' His voice was stern; he was in control again. Caitlin sank into the nearest chair and rested her arms on the kitchen table.

Connor paced the floor. "Look," he finally said. "What's going on between you and Tony Black?"

Caitlin was dumbfounded. "Tony? Nothing!" she exclaimed. "Actually, I can't stand him. He's creepy!"

Connor whirled to face her. "Is that the truth? I have to know." His eyes were the color of winter clouds over Storm King Mountain.

Caitlin's eyes narrowed. "What right do you have to question my integrity?" she snapped. "I've never lied to you and I never will. When I say there's nothing between Tony and me, you can believe it, mister! Not that it's any of your business."

She jumped to her feet, and Connor caught her close. Her breathing was ragged, and she was sure he could feel her heart thumping against his chest. She tried to pull away from his grip. "Let me go! What do you think you're doing?" she gritted out between clenched teeth.

"I'm doing this." For the second time that night she lost herself in his kiss.

An eternity later, he released her. She staggered and sat down suddenly, vaguely thankful that a chair happened to be under her.

"That's why I needed to know about Tony." His husky voice sent shivers up her back. "I couldn't stand the thought of you with him."

She was confused. "Why would you think I was with him?"

Connor ran his strong fingers through his hair. "While I was in Denver, I ran into Tony in the hotel lounge. I didn't ask what he was doing there; I just assumed it was business. Of course, you can't just ignore a neighbor when you're away from home, so I bought him a drink and we started talking, even though I normally wouldn't pick him as a drinking buddy.

"It wasn't too long before he pulled a black velvet box out of his jacket pocket and showed me a pretty impressive diamond ring." Connor's voice broke and he cleared his throat before continuing.

"He said it was for you."

"For me!"

"Yeah. That's kind of how I reacted. It just stunned me. He said you'd been seeing each other for quite a while and that he'd come to Denver mainly to buy you an engagement ring. He was so . . . cocky. I just wanted to punch him!" Connor smacked a fist on the countertop. "I don't know how I controlled myself. I'd been building all these fantasies about you and me, and here this sleaze was telling me you were going to marry him."

"No way!" Caitlin jumped up. "We've never had an understanding. He did ask me to marry him, but I certainly didn't agree, and I never will!" The blood rushed to her face, giving her the appearance of an angry angel. Connor could barely restrain himself from kissing her again. But he sensed that moving too quickly would have a worse impact than sending her and Tony on an all-expense-paid trip to Hawaii.

He laid a gentle hand on her shoulder. "Cait, I'm here for you, no matter what. I just wanted you to know that. I'll leave now. No, don't say anything." He laid a finger against her lips. "I'll be back soon." His lips grazed hers and then he was gone.

The door swung shut behind him, and Caitlin shivered from the night air. Or so she told herself.

Chapter Fourteen

"Come on, Jeff. You've got three trail riders rarin' to go." Caitlin banged on Jeff's door at six-thirty the next morning.

The closed door muffled his reply. Cait shrugged and went downstairs.

She fixed him a quick breakfast of scrambled eggs, ham, and warmed-up muffins. Unlike their guests, Jeff needed fuel first thing in the morning.

Jeff had the horses saddled and ready in the corral by the time the Norrises and Mr. West came out of the guest house. Caitlin watched from the kitchen window as they swung onto the horses and trotted out into the pasture. Jeff was taking them to the spring that gave the operation its name.

Caitlin sang softly to herself as she chopped walnuts and stirred up the batter for a coffee cake. It should be ready by the time the riders got back, and hot coffee cake would go well with the cheese omelets she planned to serve for breakfast. She'd prepare everything beforehand and then quickly cook the omelets on the stove in the common room.

Around nine o'clock she saw the riders approaching. The stove timer went off, and she set the steaming coffee cake on the wooden cutting board near the sink. The eggs waited in the refrigerator, already beaten. She finished shredding the cheese and put the food on a tray and covered it with a clean dish towel, then carefully carried it to the guesthouse.

Mrs. West wasn't in the common room, and Caitlin hoped she was still sleeping. She'd rather not deal with the unpleasant woman alone. She lighted the stove burner and set the omelet pan on it to heat. She'd have to pick up another pan the next time she was in town. One omelet at a time was all right when there were only a few guests, but if they filled up, it would take too long to feed eight people.

She poured a portion of egg mixture into the pan and let it simmer while she set the table. By the time the table was set, it was time to add the cheese, and the riders came trooping in from the ranch yard.

"Something smells wonderful," Mrs. Norris said as she washed her hands at the kitchen sink.

"The coffee cake's on the table, and I've got an omelet about ready," Caitlin replied. "Help yourselves to the cake."

She slid the omelet onto Mrs. Norris's plate and poured more eggs into the pan.

"I'll see if Karen's up," Mr. West said.

"Here, honey. I'll split this omelet with you, and then you can give me part of yours." Mrs. Norris cut the egg dish and slid half of it onto her husband's plate.

"Thanks, hon." Mr. Norris cut two large pieces of coffee cake and handed one to his wife.

Mr. West returned just as the second omelet was ready to eat. He brought his plate over to the stove, and Caitlin served him.

"I'll have another ready for Mrs. West in just a couple of minutes," she said.

"It'll take her longer than that to get dressed," he

replied. "In fact, don't even start hers until you see the whites of her eyes." He chuckled at the joke.

"Okay. I'll fix the Norrises' other one," Caitlin said.

While the omelet cooked, she poured the remaining coffee into Mrs. Norris's cup and started a new pot.

"Do you want me to split it for you?" she asked as she brought the finished omelet to the table.

"Thanks. Just give me about a third of it," Mrs. Norris said. "Ken can have the rest."

"And just when can I have mine?" Mrs. West's voice interrupted the casual talk. She stood in the doorway, elegantly attired in a white silk jumpsuit and red sandals. Her hair was immaculate and her makeup flawless. Caitlin wondered how she could look so good and act so miserable.

"I'll start yours right away," she said. "It'll only take a couple of minutes. Go ahead and have some coffee cake." She smiled at Mrs. West as she passed her on the way to the stove, but her effort at friendliness was wasted. The woman ignored her and sat down at the table, after making a big show of dusting off the seat of her chair. Caitlin fumed at this implied criticism of her housekeeping.

As soon as Mrs. West was served, Caitlin loaded her tray with the cooking dishes and went back to the house. Normally she'd do the washing up in the sink in the guesthouse, but she wasn't up to having that woman make any more snide remarks about Spring Hollow Guest Ranch.

A little after ten, the men carried their luggage out to the car, and the women climbed into the backseat. Mr. Norris came across the yard to pay for the rooms while Mr. West settled himself behind the steering wheel.

"Thanks for everything. We really had a great time,"

Mr. Norris said as he handed Caitlin the money to pay for their stay.

"Thank you for coming," she replied. "We love having new people visit us. If you're ever up this way again, stop in."

"Oh, we will," he declared. "This is one of the nicest places we've ever stayed, no matter what Karen says. I hope you weren't offended by her."

Caitlin laughed. "I learned very early that you can't please everyone. I'm just glad the rest of you had a good time."

She waved to them as they pulled out, and Mr. and Mrs. Norris waved back. Mrs. West stared stonily ahead, ignoring the last gesture of hospitality.

Jeff and Linnie came out of the living room.

"Where have you been?" Caitlin asked.

"Hiding out," Jeff said. "We didn't want to run into ol' Prune Face."

"Thank goodness she's gone," Linnie added.

"Well, sit down, kids. I baked an extra coffee cake for us." Caitlin cut the pastry into squares and poured glasses of milk.

"Did you get the horses brushed and put away?" she asked.

"Yeah. I did all that while you were cooking," he replied. "No way did I want to see Mrs. West again. I figured she'd never come near a stable."

"You figured right," Caitlin said. "It's too bad she's such a sourpuss. We only had to put up with her for a few hours. Her husband has to put up with her all the time."

"Do you think we'll have many people as awful as her?" Linnie asked.

"I hope not!" Caitlin's exclamation was heartfelt.

"But even if we do, we have to be nice to them. That's what we're in business for. You guys don't have to deal with them. I'll take all the flak. If we get another one like her, just pull your disappearing act whenever you can."

"Okay. I'll stick to stuff I know, like horses," Jeff said.

As Caitlin did the dishes, her thoughts wandered from Mrs. West to the lights in the pasture to Connor Devlin. She'd have to mention the mysterious lights to him the next time he came by. Her hands slowed as she recalled last night's events, and she willed him to appear, but he evidently wasn't tuned in to her wavelength. *So much for ESP,* she thought. *But I can wait. I can wait.*

Chapter Fifteen

As word spread of the superb accommodations and food, reservations flooded in. By the middle of June, there was hardly an empty bed for the rest of the summer. Caitlin amused herself by projecting the income of Spring Hollow and was relieved to find that the first and second installments of the loan could be repaid by the end of August. And if the hunters came in the numbers that the Department of Fish and Game expected, she'd be able to make the land payment, too.

Jeff kept busy with trail rides, and Linnie earned extra money by baby-sitting children when their parents wanted a night on the town or just to be alone for a few hours. Caitlin juggled the work of cooking, cleaning (with Linnie's help), and keeping the books for the business, as well as ordering supplies. Even their well-stocked freezer and large garden couldn't keep up with the demands of six to eight extra people every day.

Connor dropped by occasionally, but Caitlin was too busy or too tired to consider kindling a romance. He, too, was involved in lengthy business discussions that required his presence in Denver almost weekly. Tony stayed away from the ranch. Caitlin saw him only in passing, at the store in town or driving by on the road. She was glad he had other things to occupy him. She didn't relish being the object of his attention again. Thus the summer passed in a blur of work and sweat and weariness.

Soon the families with children dwindled as the opening day of school crept nearer. Jeff reluctantly went into town with Caitlin to shop for school clothes.

"I sure wish I could stay at the ranch," he complained. "The law says you only have to finish eighth grade, and I did that ages ago. I could drop out now."

"And by my law, you'd better not even think about it," his sister said sternly. "People think that someone who drops out of school is a big fat zero. You'll never get a job without a diploma. And besides, school's not that hard for you. You've always gotten good grades, so why do you want to drop out?"

Jeff wriggled uncomfortably. "Aw, I guess I don't, really. It's just that I hate to see you and Linnie doing all the work this fall. It's just not fair that you two have to bust your buns while I lounge around a classroom all day."

Caitlin gave him a quick hug, much to his chagrin. "You just worry about your grades. Linnie and I will worry about the ranch. Besides, the business is slowing down some. There'll still be plenty for you to do when you get home. Take a study hall and use it. You might not have much time for homework," she advised.

"Okay, but three years seems like a long time," he muttered.

"It'll fly by. Pretty soon you'll be like Linnie, wondering where the time went."

She paid for the purchases and they went out to the parking lot.

"Can I drive, Cait?" Jeff pleaded. "I almost have my learner's permit."

She shook her head. "You'll just have to wait another

two months. I'd hate to get busted for letting you drive without a permit.'' She got behind the wheel, and Jeff settled grouchily into the passenger's seat. She struggled to keep a straight face as he sank low in the seat, crossing his arms across his stomach and scowling.

''Better fasten your seat belt,'' she said without looking at him. She snapped her own into place.

Without speaking, he straightened up and clasped his.

His bad mood didn't last long, and soon they were chattering away about the ranch, school, and myriad other subjects. Caitlin's attention strayed; she was so used to driving this route that she felt she could do it in her sleep. She drove casually, one arm on the edge of the window, the other steering the truck down the gravel road that wound the last five miles to the ranch. The road was dry, and the pickup kicked up a trail of dust as they barreled along the narrow road. Caitlin noticed a plume of dust billowing up from the top of the rise just ahead and slowed down, steering over to the far right side of the road. This wasn't a place to be meeting someone head-on.

A huge cattle-hauling truck topped the rise, right in the center of the road. Caitlin slowed more and edged closer to the steep embankment. The semi bore down on them. She honked desperately, trying to alert the driver to their presence, but to no avail.

The truck loomed closer, and she had only a split second to react. She twisted the steering wheel to the right and the pickup left the road. She and Jeff were thrown against their seat belts as the blue truck slid down the grass-covered embankment into the ditch. The rear end slewed downhill, preventing them from rolling, and the pickup came to rest against a fence post.

Caitlin automatically reached for the key and shut off

the engine. Dust settled down upon them and she coughed. They were both too stunned to speak.

Finally she said, ''Are you all right?''

''Yeah, I guess so,'' Jeff replied.

They unhooked their seat belts, and Caitlin shoved hard against her door. It squealed open, and she climbed out. Jeff followed her, as his side of the truck was shoved tight against the fence. They stood in the ditch, watching the dust settle and listening to the fading sound of the semi's engine as it whined into the distance.

''He didn't even slow down!'' Jeff was flabbergasted. ''Why didn't he stop?''

''I don't have any idea,'' Caitlin said as she began to clamber up the steep slope. The drying weed stems were harsh under her fingers as she pulled herself up onto the road. Jeff followed on her heels. They stood in the road, looking back toward town, where a vanishing dust trail marked the cattle truck's passing.

''Well, there's no point in standing around here,'' she said. ''It's only a couple of miles to the ranch. Let's start walking.''

The gravel on the road rolled under their feet as they trudged up the hill. The sun burned mercilessly, and Caitlin wished for something to drink. *Just get on with it,* she thought grimly. *There's no water between here and home.*

Dirt boiled into the sky to the west, and the sound of an engine came to them. They stepped to the side of the road, and Jeff waved at the approaching vehicle.

''It's Mr. Devlin!'' Jeff shouted as the Blazer skidded to a stop.

''What're you two doing on foot?'' Connor asked as he stepped down from the cab.

"Some son of a—er . . ." Jeff's voice dwindled at Caitlin's stern look.

She continued. "A cattle truck just ran us off the road. He came over the rise, right in the middle of the road. I had to hit the ditch to keep from a head-on collision. And the driver didn't even slow down, much less stop!" Her anger was plain.

Connor grabbed her and held her against him, smoothing her hair with his hand. "Oh, Cait! I almost lost you!" he whispered savagely. She could feel him trembling. Suddenly the shock caught up with her and she sagged in his embrace.

"Cait!" Jeff cried.

"It's okay," she managed to say. Connor eased her into the open door of the Blazer and she leaned against the seat, her eyes closed.

"Is she okay?" Jeff asked Connor.

"I think it's just shock," he replied. "She should be better in a minute." She opened her eyes and took comfort in his look and the warmth of his hand on her shoulder.

"Where's the truck?"

"Down there." Jeff pointed back the way they'd come.

Connor said, "Climb in. I've got a tow strap in the back end. Maybe we can pull it out, if it's not damaged too badly."

Jeff scrambled into the passenger's side of the Blazer, and Caitlin slid across the seat toward her brother so that Connor could get behind the wheel. His solid strength radiated from him as he put the car into gear and drove toward the site of the wreck.

He pulled the Blazer off onto the shoulder and the three got out. They half slid, half ran down the ditch bank to the blue pickup. All the tires seemed to be sound, and there didn't appear to be any damage to the frame. Connor knelt and examined the undercarriage, then stood up.

"I think we can get 'er pulled out," he said. "Jeff, get the yellow tow strap out of the back and toss one end down here."

Jeff scuttled up the slope to obey. Soon Connor had the tough nylon strap secured to the front bumper of the truck. "You steer," he said to Caitlin. "I'll pull as easily as I can. If you feel anything strange, honk and I'll stop."

She nodded agreement and settled behind the wheel while he climbed up and secured the other end of the strap to the trailer hitch on the Blazer.

Jeff stood well clear, keeping an eye on the strap and both vehicles as Connor eased the Blazer forward. The pickup jolted as it began the ascent, and Caitlin's knuckles were white on the steering wheel, her lips tight and thin as she concentrated on steering up the bank. In a few minutes the truck was once again upright on the road.

Jeff hurried to undo the strap while Connor called back, "See if it'll start."

Caitlin turned the key, and the engine roared to life. She put the truck in gear and steered to the side of the road. Everything seemed to be working well, no problems with the steering or tires that she could detect.

"I'll follow you back to the ranch," Connor shouted, and motioned for Jeff to get into the Blazer.

Caitlin drove slowly at first, but picked up speed as her confidence increased. By the time they pulled into the ranch yard, she was over the worst of the experience.

Jeff and Connor followed her into the house, and she poured iced tea for them all.

"Jeff tells me he couldn't see any markings on the truck," Connor said. "No name on the door, nothing."

"That's right. Pretty strange, now that I think of it," she replied. "Most trucking companies have their name and logo on the cab."

Linnie came in from the guest house, where she'd just finished the housekeeping chores. Jeff hurried to explain their latest adventure, while Connor went to phone the sheriff.

Caitlin followed him into the living room. "Do you think there's any point?" she asked him. "The driver's miles away by now, and we have no way of identifying him."

"I know, but it has to be reported, if only for insurance purposes," he replied.

Caitlin spoke to a sheriff's deputy, briefly outlining the afternoon's events, then hung up.

"He said there's no point in coming out, but for us to have the truck checked over by a mechanic. He took down the information and will file a report."

She collapsed into her mother's armchair and ran her fingers through her hair. It felt gritty from the road dust. She giggled wildly and then burst into tears as she thought of how much worse the day could have ended than in dirty hair.

Connor sank to his knees beside her and held her close while she cried. He crooned nonsense in her ear as if she were a child to be comforted after waking from a nightmare. Slowly her sobs decreased, and she took the handkerchief he offered and blew her nose.

"Has anything else strange happened lately?" he asked when she'd regained her composure.

"Strange?" She looked at him. "You don't think this is related to our other troubles, do you? It was just an accident."

"An accident that could have killed you and Jeff," he

said grimly. "What would have happened to the ranch then?"

His words chilled her. She carried no life insurance, had no will. Linnie would have been left on her own, possibly homeless.

"No! I can't believe that someone would try to kill me!" She jumped up and paced the living room. "The ranch isn't worth anything to anyone except us. The bank would take it for payment on the loan I took out to finance the guesthouse. No one would gain anything."

"No one?" he asked.

"No one," she replied emphatically. "It was an accident, pure and simple. All the same, I'm going to see Mr. Hirsch right away and make arrangements for Linnie and Jeff if anything should happen to me."

"Good idea. Are you all right?" he asked.

"I'm fine now," she said as they went back to the kitchen.

Linnie hugged her sister tightly. "I'm so glad you didn't get hurt!" she exclaimed.

"Me too," Caitlin said.

"I have to be getting into town," Connor announced. "I have some business that can't wait until tomorrow."

Caitlin followed him to the Blazer. "Thanks for rescuing us," she said. "I don't know what we would have done if you hadn't come along."

"You'd have managed somehow," he said with a smile. "You're a survivor." He started the car.

She waved as he drove away, thankful for his strength, his caring, his ready presence in times of trouble.

Chapter Sixteen

School started the last week of August, and Caitlin drove Jeff into town without incident.

She dropped Jeff off in front of the high school. "Remember, you have to catch the bus home," she warned.

"I know," he grumbled. "I sure wish I was sixteen. Then I could drive in. It's not like I don't know how."

"You're an excellent driver," Caitlin assured him, "but the law's the law. Until April, you're stuck on the bus."

She waved and pulled away from the curb. Students hurried everywhere, greeting each other after the summer separation. The morning air flowed warmly into the truck through the open window, and Caitlin took a deep breath, savoring the remnants of summer.

Already, in the high country, the grasses had headed out and the shrubs were taking on the rich purple and red hues of fall. Snow could come at any time in the higher elevations, but Caitlin hoped it would hold off for a couple of months. Winter lasted a long time. She wanted to enjoy autumn.

The second loan installment wasn't due until October, but the summer had been so successful that she could make the payment and save some interest by paying early. Mr. Faraday met her in the bank lobby. "I hear you've had quite a summer," he said.

"Yes, we've done quite well," she replied. "In fact, I'd like to pay the second installment on the loan."

Mr. Faraday was taken aback. "Why, that's wonderful. I had no idea your summer had gone that well." He seated Caitlin in the green velvet chair in front of the desk. "But are you sure you're not going to run short of money, paying ahead like this? Your land payment's due the first of November."

Caitlin held up a hand. "I know, Mr. Faraday. We're going to make that payment on time, too. Quite a few people have made reservations for September, and I've got several thousand dollars in savings, besides what I'm paying today. And this way, I save on the interest." She grinned at him as she handed him the check.

He took it and said, "I'll get you a receipt. I'm so glad that things are working out for you. We all worried about you after the accident." He hurried away to the teller's cage.

His words started an ache in her heart, but it was bearable. Time had taken the edge off her loss, but it would be a long time before she could think about her parents without wanting to cry. To distract herself, she looked around the lobby.

Connor Devlin entered, and she half rose to greet him. His eyes lit up at the sight of her, and he hurried over to take the seat next to her.

"Cait! You're looking well. Hard work must agree with you." He took her hand in his. Her skin warmed under his touch. The attraction was as powerful as ever, but she strove to keep the atmosphere casual.

"It must." She laughed. "And how about you? Seems like we haven't seen each other forever."

He shrugged. "Business as usual."

"I'll tell you what. Why don't you come to dinner

some night? It's slowed down enough that I don't have to play superhostess. How about next Wednesday?''

He smiled. ''Wednesday. At six.''

Mr. Faraday returned and handed Caitlin her receipt. ''Hello, Connor. Good to see you again,'' he said. ''I'll be right with you.''

''Thanks, Mr. Faraday,'' Caitlin said as she slipped the receipt into her purse. ''I'll see you in November with the land payment.''

She had to restrain herself from skipping out of the bank. The loan payment was made, Connor was coming to dinner, and the world basked in sunshine.

The days dragged as Caitlin waited for Wednesday to arrive. She kept busy with guests and routine chores, but she thought almost constantly of the upcoming dinner with Connor.

At last Wednesday dawned, cool and clear. Caitlin scouted through her wardrobe, trying to find something to wear that evening. ''Oh, it's hopeless!'' she exclaimed.

''What is?'' Linnie leaned in the doorway.

''My clothes. I don't have anything to wear. Why didn't I take time to go buy something nice?'' Caitlin moaned as she flopped onto the bed. ''I hate my clothes!''

Linnie sat on the bed next to her sister. ''How about—'' she began, but Caitlin interrupted her.

''I don't want to hear *about!* I've tried everything and nothing works. I'm sick of it. I wish I'd never invited him!'' She threw herself back onto the bed and pounded the mattress.

Linnie stood up. ''Don't worry about it. Something will work out,'' she said. ''Can you get along without me for a few hours? I have some projects I want to finish.''

''Sure,'' Caitlin replied, her brief fit of the sulks over. She smiled at her sister and started stuffing clothes back into her dresser and closet. ''I can clean the rooms myself, and we don't get our next group until late this afternoon. Take all the time you need. You've worked hard this summer, and you deserve a day to yourself.''

''Thanks, Cait. And don't worry about the clothes. Connor will love you no matter what you wear.'' Her expression was unreadable as she left her sister.

Linnie disappeared into the spare room that served as a catchall. It was where they sewed, did the ironing, and stored everything that didn't go somewhere else. Soon the sound of the sewing machine hummed through the house.

Caitlin filled the hours cleaning the guesthouse and planning the evening meal. The evenings were still nice enough to cook and eat outside, and the guests enjoyed the chance to picnic without the work involved. Caitlin cut up chickens for barbecuing and stirred together a spicy rice casserole. She assembled everything for a wilted spinach salad, except the spinach. She'd pick that just before suppertime. She split two chocolate cakes into four layers and spread whipped cream between and over the layers, then sprinkled the whole thing with nuts and cherries.

Jeff arrived just as she was putting the finishing touches on the cake. ''Can I lick the bowl?'' he asked.

''Sure.'' Caitlin handed him the beaters and the bowl that held the remnants of the whipped cream, and he settled back to enjoy it. For a minute, Caitlin saw him as he was when he was six and begging for the bowl. *So long ago,* she thought, *and so much has happened since then.*

Linnie interrupted her reverie as she burst into the kitchen. "You'd better get ready, Cait. It's almost five. I'll finish up while you shower."

"Thanks. You just need to pick some spinach and mix the wilt." Caitlin hurried up to the bathroom and ran the water until it steamed. The shower felt good, hot and relaxing. She shampooed her hair and let the water wash away her grime and tensions. Reluctantly she turned off the steaming spray and toweled off, wishing she had something to wear that would impress Connor, wishing she were taller and prettier, wishing she were anyone but her ordinary self. "Oh, quit feeling sorry for yourself," she admonished herself out loud. "Get your act together. There's not much time left."

She swathed herself in her old bathrobe and dried her hair. Fortunately her short, swingy haircut didn't need setting. A quick blowing with the hair dryer and it fell into place. She leaned close to the mirror, darkening her brown eyes with liner and mascara. Her eyes were definitely her best feature. Now if she just had something to wear!

Caitlin was surprised to see Linnie in her bedroom. "I thought you were finishing dinner," she said.

"I work fast," Linnie answered. "Here. Try this on." She held up a dress of mint green chiffon. The full skirt hung in soft folds, and the bodice draped softly from a bateau neckline. The sleeves were long and full and gathered into tight cuffs.

Caitlin gasped. "Where did this come from?"

Her sister smiled. "I made it today. I was going to make it for me. It was already cut out. All I had to do was shorten it a little. We're the same size, except I'm taller. Do you like it?''

"Like it? I love it!" Caitlin hugged her sister hard. "Thank you, thank you, thank you!"

"Jeff's checking in our new group," Linnie said as she hung the dress on the closet door. "I'd better go see how he's doing."

Caitlin slipped into some lacy underwear, then pulled the dress over her head. She struggled briefly with the back zipper, and then stood silently in front of the mirror. Could that be her? The green color brought out the peach tones in her skin, and her dark eyes sparkled. The fabric draped her body, hugging it softly in all the right places. It was perfect.

She strapped on high-heeled white sandals and put on gold earrings shaped like aspen leaves. She dabbed Chanel No. 5 behind her ears and on her pulse points, then twirled in front of the mirror, watching her reflection and feeling beautiful.

Linnie and Jeff were waiting at the bottom of the stairs as she came down. "Wow! Is that you, sis?" Jeff whistled appreciatively.

"Thank you, kind sir," she said, smiling. "I feel like a princess. But how am I going to keep this clean while I cook?"

"You're not cooking. I am," Linnie said. "In fact, you're not even to come outside." She led the way to the formal dining room, a room used only on holidays and special occasions. Caitlin gasped.

The table had been covered with the white lace cloth their mother had had in her hope chest. Two settings of their best china and crystal gleamed in the late-afternoon sun that streamed through the lace curtains. White candles stood at attention in silver holders.

Caitlin sank into one of the dining room chairs and rested her chin on her hands. "I can't believe it," she murmured.

Jeff cleared his throat. "It's kind of our way of saying thanks for all the work you've done since Mom and Dad died. We want tonight to be special for you."

"Now don't cry," Linnie cautioned. "You'll ruin your makeup. Oh! There's Mr. Devlin."

Caitlin brushed at the tears that had gathered in her eyes, jumped up, and followed her brother and sister into the kitchen. Jeff opened the door before Caitlin's guest could knock.

"Hello," Connor said.

"Excuse us," Linnie said as she picked up the tray of chicken pieces and went outside. Jeff followed her with the barbecue sauce.

"Was it something I said?" Connor asked as he looked after them in bewilderment.

"No," Caitlin said. "They've taken it upon themselves to do the cooking and serving tonight so you and I can have some time together. I hope you don't mind." She blushed, adding a becoming pink tint to her tanned cheeks.

"Not at all." Connor surveyed her, taking in her sparkling eyes, her womanly curves. "You look wonderful," he said.

"Thank you," she replied. "Come in and sit down."

"Oh, this is for you." Connor handed her a bottle of fine wine. "I thought it would go well with dinner."

"Thank you again." She smiled. "I'll just get a corkscrew." She rummaged in one of the kitchen drawers, and he had time to appreciate the way the dress hugged her waist and flared around her legs.

She led the way to the dining room and set the wine on the table. ''Do you have a match?''

Connor handed her a silver lighter, and she touched the flame to the candle wicks.

''The kids certainly went to a lot of trouble,'' he remarked.

''It was a complete surprise to me. I had no idea they were planning anything like this.''

The sun had sunk behind the mountains, and the room was bathed in soft twilight, punctuated by the golden glow of the candles. Caitlin stood at the window, which gave a good view of the barbecue grill and the people gathered around the fire.

''Can you believe I haven't even met any of the guests yet?'' she said. ''Linnie and Jeff have done everything.''

He moved closer to her and lifted the curtain. Her pulse quickened. A faint scent of aftershave drifted to her, and she longed to °pull him close and kiss him. Instead, she clasped her hands together tightly. ''I don't know what I'd do without them. They've both done more than their share of the work this summer.''

''You've all worked hard,'' he said softly. He draped his arm over her shoulder, and she shivered. She leaned forward to escape his touch, pulling the curtain aside once more to check on the group around the fire.

Jeff had left the fire and was sprinting back toward the house.

''I wonder what happened?'' Caitlin said as the back door slammed. She looked inquiringly at Connor and they turned as one.

Just as Caitlin started toward the door, Jeff appeared, bearing two salad plates on a tray. He'd draped a dish towel over his arm, and as he set the plates on the table, he said, ''Madame, monsieur, please be seated.''

Connor chuckled at the French accent Jeff had affected, but pulled out Caitlin's chair and seated her, then sat down across from her.

Jeff struggled for a moment with the wine bottle and corkscrew, then gratefully relinquished them when Connor held out a helping hand, and bowed his way out of the room. Connor handled the bottle deftly, and the cork gave a soft popping sound as he eased it out of the bottle. The golden wine sparkled as he poured it into the crystal wineglasses. He handed Caitlin her glass and sat down again.

"Here's to a lovely evening," Connor said as he raised his glass. Caitlin lifted hers and touched the rim to his. She longed to touch his hand, but she didn't trust her emotions. Instead, she let her eyes speak for her. Connor smiled and she knew that he, too, was reining in his feelings.

The candles' glow brightened as the night closed in, and they talked of inconsequential things as they ate. Jeff reappeared to take the salad plates away and serve the chicken, rice, and green beans amandine.

Connor poured more wine, and Caitlin felt her mood expand in a glorious rush of joy as he touched her hand.

"What are you planning to do this winter?" he asked.

"Just carry on as we have been," she replied. "All our rooms are completely booked during hunting season, and I even have a few reservations for cross-country skiers and snowmobilers. We won't be buying more cattle, so there's plenty of room for the snowmobilers to run in the pasture, and the skiers can roam the hills to their hearts' content."

Connor swirled the wine in his glass and frowned. "Are you sure you can make it? Things change quickly.

I'd hate to see you count on something that might not be there.''

"That sounds ominous," she said, trying to keep her tone light. "Do you know something I don't?"

"No," he admitted, "I guess I just naturally take a more serious view of life than most people."

A slight tap at the door alerted them to her brother's presence. He entered the candlelit room, bearing two plates of dessert.

"Madame, ze dezzairt iz sairved." Jeff flourished his towel as he set the portions of torte on the table.

"Thank you, waiter. That will be all." Caitlin waved him away with an imperious hand, playing the game, glad of the momentary distraction. "You may leave us now."

"*Oui,* madame." Jeff bowed himself out of the room and closed the door.

Full dark had fallen, and the candlelight left the corners of the room in shadow. Connor pushed his cake aside and stood up. Caitlin trembled under his steady gaze.

"Cait, if there's ever anything you need, all you have to do is call."

"I know," she said as she put her hand into his outstretched palm.

Even in her high heels, she barely came to his shoulder. Her eyes closed as his lips covered hers, and she swayed closer to him. He gathered her into his arms, and she went gladly. She knew then that, no matter what might happen later, she was his forever.

Chapter Seventeen

Summer slipped into autumn, and the hills blazed with scarlet scrub oak and golden aspen. Nights were frosty, but at high noon the October days held a remembrance of summer's heat. Shadows lay long and cool in the groves of spruce, and aspen leaves drifted on vagrant breezes to carpet the forest floor in hues of gold.

Caitlin loved this time of year. During September, the guesthouse had been filled nearly every day with older people who weren't tied down to their children's schedules for vacations. In addition to running the business, she and Linnie had spent a good amount of time canning and freezing the extra produce from the garden for the winter ahead. Now the bright, crisp days were perfect for riding Rough or Ready through the changing aspen groves, and the frosty nights made Caitlin thankful for the warmth of the furnace and the loaded pantry shelves. October was a peace-filled time between the labors of summer and the storms of winter.

Business at Spring Hollow had slacked off, with only the weekends bringing a houseful of guests. After the busy summer, all three Morriseys were content to rest and recuperate before the busy hunting season, which began the first day of November. They were booked solid for the hunting season, and quite a few more reservations had come in from snowmobilers and skiers, filling the old barn to capacity from the middle of December until after New Year's.

The last week of October, the weather changed. Indian summer gave way to steely skies and chill winds. There had been flurries of snow in the higher peaks throughout the month, but now it looked as though winter was settling in in earnest. The scent of snow scurried on the changing wind, and Caitlin knew that a good storm now would be just what the hunters wanted, as it would drive the deer and elk down from the mountaintops to the meadows below, making hunting easier. She had no qualms about the killing of deer and elk; her father had hunted, as had the peoples who roamed the land since the beginning of time. As a rancher's child, she had no illusions about the structure of the food chain.

The Wednesday before Halloween, Linnie wanted to go into town and do some shopping and visit friends from school who she hadn't seen all summer.

"Okay," Caitlin said, in answer to her sister's request. "You can drive Jeff in to school and then pick him up afterward. And while you're in town, will you pick up some things for me?"

She handed Linnie a list of staples they were running low on.

"Sure, Cait. Boy, this is quite a bit of stuff," she said as she looked over the list. "A hundred pounds of flour, fifty pounds of sugar . . ." Her voice trailed away.

Caitlin finished wiping the breakfast crumbs off the kitchen table and rinsed the dishcloth. "We've got a full house for the next month. And these hunters aren't going to be satisfied with snacks. They're going to need lots of food in the morning, and after a day in the mountains, supper will have to be good and hearty. In fact, I doubt these supplies will get us through the month, but it's a place to start. Next year we'll have a better idea of what we need for each season.''

Jeff stomped in from the barn and stuffed his schoolbooks into his backpack. ''You ready, Linnie? I've got a test first period,'' he said. He rubbed his hands together to warm them and added, ''I bet we have snow before dark. It's really damp out.''

Linnie zipped her parka and took the money Caitlin handed her. ''We'll be back by four-thirty or so,'' she said. ''See you then.''

The two hurried to the truck, and Caitlin watched them as they swung out of the lane onto the highway.

Then she took the bank statement that had arrived the day before into the office and got out her calculator. For an hour she checked, rechecked, and sweated over the balance. Usually this was a chore she could do the first time, but today her brain felt dead. When she'd come up with the third wrong answer, she threw her pencil down in disgust.

''I give up!'' she said with a growl. ''Either the bank messed up or I did. I just can't figure out where.''

She stood and stretched, then went to the kitchen for another cup of coffee, vowing to deal with the checkbook later. She sat down and leaned back in the chair, watching the steam rise from the coffee cup, thinking of nothing. For months she'd been so busy planning and worrying and solving problems that she hadn't had time for the luxury of just sitting and staring into space.

She poured a second cup of coffee and wandered through the house, picking up clutter and straightening the house. She put a load of laundry in the washer and sorted the clean clothes that had piled up in the laundry basket. She tried to mend the knee of a pair of Jeff's jeans, but her fingers were clumsy and the thread knotted under her touch. She threw down the pants in disgust and resumed her wandering.

The sky loomed dark above the ranch, and noon seemed like evening. Caitlin blamed her unsettled feeling on the weather. Whenever the barometer fell, so did her spirits. She prowled the house, peering from the windows, looking for any stray flakes of snow, but the clouds only sank lower over the peaks.

Finally she couldn't stand being cooped up longer. She changed into riding boots and pulled a heavy sweater over her turtleneck. She zipped her yellow parka and checked the pockets to make sure she had her gloves, and then she left the house.

The big barn was warm and dark and silent, except for the occasional rustle of straw as the horses moved in their stalls. She flipped on the light in the tack room and hauled out Ready's saddle and bridle.

"Come on, old boy. You and I are going to get some exercise," she said as she laid the Indian saddle blanket on his back and heaved the heavy Western saddle up. His large, dark eyes seemed to question why she'd want to leave a perfectly good warm barn to ride into a gathering storm, but he only snorted and let her slip the bit between his teeth.

A chill wind moaned low around the eaves and whistled mournfully through the corral rails as she led the chestnut out into the yard. She almost turned back, but Ready had his head up, sniffing the wind, catching the wildness of the day. His mood now matched hers, and he tugged at the reins eagerly.

She fastened the barn door, pulled on her leather gloves, and swung into the saddle. "Let's go, boy." She nudged him with her knees and guided him into the north pasture. He needed no urging now to stretch out and run.

Tears stung Caitlin's eyes as the cold wind whipped past her face. Her dark hair was tossed around her cheeks by the speed of her ride, and she wished she'd worn her cap. Then she forgot her discomfort in the sheer exhilaration of pounding across the flat, brown grass toward the looming bulk of Storm King Mountain.

They pushed on up the flank of the mountain. Ready slowed as the land rose more steeply and the trees closed in around them. An aspen grove that had gleamed golden in the sunlight of the previous week now stood stark and almost bereft of leaves in the dismal light of a fading afternoon. Dry leaves crunched under Ready's hooves as she guided him between the somber white trunks and on across the mountainside. The spring that had inspired the name of the guest ranch lay half a mile farther on, and Caitlin decided to ride up and see if there were any fresh deer tracks around.

The small hollow that held the spring dipped into the hillside, and moss-covered granite boulders leaned against each other in a semicircle several yards across behind the seep. An earthen basin lined with stones caught the water as it welled from the ground, and a trickle of icy, clear water spilled from the lip of the pool. The tiny rivulet wandered a few yards down the hill before it disappeared into the ground. Caitlin ground-tethered Ready, letting the reins hang free, and knelt beside the small pool. The pure water reflected the dark sky and Caitlin's face as she took off a glove to scoop some of the pure springwater into her mouth. The icy water shocked her throat, and she shivered as she wiped her hand on her jeans and stood up.

She never heard him coming. She pushed herself to her feet and bumped into Tony Black as she turned to go back to Ready.

"Oh! You startled me," she exclaimed as she flinched away from him.

"Did I?" Tony's eyes were dark and hard as he looked at her. There was no remnant of the sheepish, little-boy look he'd maintained in their previous encounters. Instead, he reminded Caitlin of a cougar about to leap on an unsuspecting deer. She took an involuntary step backward and slipped on the wet bank of the spring. She stumbled, off balance. He caught her wrist and pulled her to him.

"Tony! You're hurting me," she said as his grip tightened.

"You're not hurting yet," he replied, his voice menacing, "but you will be."

"What do you mean?" Caitlin tugged futilely against his grip.

"I've waited a long time to get you alone," he said as he gave her wrist a vicious little twist. "Now you'll be out of my way forever." He smiled, and the smile was worse than the look of hatred in his eyes.

"I don't understand," she whispered. Her eyes widened. The pain in her wrist faded as fear clamped itself around her heart.

"Your father wouldn't sell the ranch to me, and you wouldn't sell either, but when you're gone, your sister and brother will be glad to take any offer I make. They won't want to stay in a place with such tragic memories." He laughed low in his throat. "It'll all be mine."

"What will all be yours? The land? You don't need more land," Caitlin said. She was genuinely bewildered.

"I don't care about the land," he said with a snarl. "It's the treasure! I've spent years tracking down the original map and piecing the clues together. And now I know exactly where it is! And no one is going to stop me from taking it. No one!''

He jerked her roughly toward the spring and shoved her down on one of the mossy boulders that lined the hollow. ''Don't move. It won't do you any good,'' he ordered. He pulled a well-worn piece of paper from inside his coat and began poring over it.

Caitlin wrapped her arms around herself, holding on to what little courage she had. She felt the damp chill of the rock seeping through her jeans and freezing her legs. Tony's expression was that of a madman. She sat as still as the stone, not daring to upset him.

A few wisps of fog drifted through the trees and curled around the edges of the hollow like cold smoke. Soon the grove would be blotted out by the autumn mist. If she were patient, perhaps she could also disappear into the fog. Then she might have a chance to escape this maniac who was her neighbor. Caitlin shifted on the rock, but his piercing look stopped her.

''Don't even think about trying to run,'' he said. ''You wouldn't get far.'' He reached inside his coat again and pulled out a hunting knife. He moved closer; his leg pressed against her knee. The knife blade gleamed like tarnished silver in the stormy light as he pressed it against her stomach. She tried to pull away from the blade, but her back was tight against the boulder behind her. Her only chance to keep him from hurting her was to distract him.

''Tony—'' Her voice cracked. She cleared her throat and tried again. ''Tony, what treasure are you talking about?''

He sneered and his face twisted with anger. ''Come on, Cait, don't act stupid. You're smarter than that. The Spanish treasure, of course,'' he said.

"But Tony, that's just a legend, a folktale," she protested.

The knife pressed harder, and she flattened herself against the rock, drawing in her stomach so the blade wouldn't penetrate. The fog drifted closer. Some of the tree trunks had already disappeared in the mist.

"No, it's not," he said. "I've found the cave. I know exactly where it is. And as soon as you're out of the way, I'll be rich! It's taken months, but I'm finally going to be a millionaire."

"What do you mean, months?" she asked. His wild words bewildered her.

"With your parents out of the way, I was sure you'd sell out to me. I had a friend call with a phony company name, but you wouldn't sell to Forrest-American either." He looked at her sadly. "I even offered to marry you. You should have taken that offer instead of falling in love with Connor Devlin." He leaned closer, and she felt the fabric of the padded jacket tear under the pressure of the knife blade. "You'd still be alive tomorrow."

"You're not going to kill me!" Caitlin closed her eyes against the dizziness that engulfed her. She mustn't faint, not now.

"Of course I am. What's one more murder?"

Her eyes flew open. "One *more*? You mean—"

"I arranged that 'accident' that killed your parents. Your father was stubborn, like you. He wouldn't even talk to me about selling." He spoke casually, as though killing a person were no more important than taking cattle to market to be slaughtered.

Tears stung Caitlin's eyes, and she lunged toward him, ignoring the sharp pain that stabbed through her side. "You killed my parents? You . . ."

He slapped her hard, knocking her back onto the rock,

then looked dispassionately at the blade in his hand. "Keep that up and I won't have to kill you. You'll do it yourself," he snapped. "Almost like your parents did. All it took was a loose fence post and a stray cow spooked into the road at the right time."

Caitlin rubbed her cheek, which now bore the imprint of his hand. "I suppose you set fire to the guesthouse, too," she said. The anger in her voice seemed to amuse him.

"Sure. If your brat of a brother hadn't been prowling around, I'd have put you out of business before you got started. And you're probably wondering what happened to that cattle truck that ran you off the road last summer."

"You?" By this time, Caitlin wasn't surprised at anything Tony said.

"Of course. You and your brother are too darn lucky."

"And you were the trespasser in the north pasture last March."

He smiled. "Sure. I'd found the map by then, and I didn't want anyone to see me sneaking around your property. It's my bad luck you had to take a walk in that blizzard, but fortunately I got out before the cops arrived. In fact, if any of my 'accidents' had gone off as planned, I'd have had the gold a long time ago."

"So where *is* the treasure?" she asked. "If you're going to kill me anyway, it won't hurt to tell me."

Tony chuckled. For a moment, his handsome mouth smiling, his dark eyes sparkling, he looked like the old Tony, carefree happy, everybody's friend.

"You're sitting on it!" He doubled over and whooped with laughter.

Caitlin slid down from her perch and stared at the rock. "What?"

"Yep, right under that boulder," he said. "Look." He

spread the paper out on the rock, too proud of his cleverness to watch Caitlin closely. "See, I traced the original map. Now here's Storm King." He pointed to a spot on the map.

Caitlin's eyes followed his finger. Then she shivered and looked up toward the mountain, now completely engulfed in fog.

"And see? Here's the cave. And it's right behind the spring. All I have to do is clear a couple of these boulders out of the way, and the treasure is mine! But first there's you to take care of." Tony turned and raised the knife. He smiled once more, like the Tony she'd known since childhood. "Don't worry, Cait. It'll be quick. I don't want you to suffer." The smile faded, and his eyes reflected the madness of his mind.

"No," she whispered. She stepped backward, edging away from the crazed killer. He stepped toward her, reaching out to hold her still for the fatal stroke.

"No!" She screamed and turned to run, but her foot caught in a fallen limb, and she fell heavily, facedown.

"Tony!" Connor Devlin's shout filled the hollow.

Caitlin rolled over into a crouching position just as Connor threw himself at Tony in a flying tackle. Tony went down under the onslaught but instinctively brought the knife up. The blade sank deep into Connor's arm. Connor ignored the blow and slammed his right fist into Tony's face. Tony's head snapped back, and he slumped, unconscious, on the ground. The fight was over almost before it began.

Caitlin scrambled to her feet. "Connor, are you all right?" she cried as she knelt beside him.

He grimaced. "I think so."

"Let me look." She unbuttoned his heavy wool coat and slipped the sleeve off his arm. The knife had slid along his biceps, tearing his shirt and leaving a thin gash on his arm. A trickle of blood soaked the plaid flannel.

He glanced at the wound. "I'm glad I wore my heavy coat," he said. "It took most of the force."

"But we have to bandage it," she protested as he pulled his coat back on.

"Just let it bleed," he said. "That'll wash out the wound. It'll quit bleeding in a few minutes."

Caitlin's legs gave way and she slumped to the ground. "What's the matter, Cait?" he asked.

"He—he tried to kill me," she stammered. Tears trickled from Caitlin's eyes, not from pain but from shock. Connor took her in his arms and rocked her gently as she sobbed. He smoothed her hair and murmured nonsense to her as if she were a child. She hiccuped and pulled away from him.

"I need a hankie," she said with a sniff, wiping her nose on her jacket sleeve.

He smiled down at her, and Caitlin's heart lurched. He gently rubbed her cheeks, wiping the tears away.

She fumbled in her pocket and came up with a battered tissue and blew her nose. "How did you know I was here?" she asked, looking up at him.

"I was riding fence and saw you racing across the pasture. I thought something had happened, so I cut across the mountain to catch you. Unfortunately the fog came down and I lost sight of you. Then I heard you scream. I saw Tony pushing the knife at you, but I couldn't do anything while he was so close. When you started to run I had my chance."

"Thank goodness you were out checking fence," she said. "I'd be dead now if it weren't for you."

"I've checked a lot of fence since . . . the accident," he said, his expression grim.

Bitterness welled up in Caitlin. "It was no accident," she said, her voice tight with anger. "Tony admitted that he let the fence down and drove your cow out into the road just as Mom and Dad came around that curve. He murdered them." She stared stonily at Tony's unconscious form.

Connor stared at her, his expression shocked. Then he helped her to her feet. "I've got rope in my saddlebags. Let's make sure he doesn't run off."

She leaned against a tree trunk for support as he disappeared into the mist. The mountain was eerily quiet, until she heard Connor's muffled steps as he made his way through the fog, leading Ready and his own horse. He cut off a length of rope from the bundle in his saddlebag, and in a few minutes Tony was trussed hand and foot.

They stood looking at his unconscious form. "I'd just as soon leave him here to rot," Connor said, "but I suppose we'd better take him along. Are you all right to ride?"

"I'm fine," Caitlin said. "It's quit bleeding and doesn't hurt at all. Okay, it hurts a little," she said in reply to his skeptical look. "But I want to see if there's really a cave here. The price has been paid. Let's see what my parents bought with their lives."

She pointed to the boulder Tony had indicated. Connor took the lasso from his saddle horn and looped it over the boulder. He tied the other end to the saddle horn.

"Stand back," he warned as he led his horse forward. Caitlin backed up several yards. The rope tightened and the animal strained harder, his breath coming in cloudy snorts as his master urged him on.

"I think it's moving!" she exclaimed.

Suddenly the rock pulled free from its centuries-old

bed. Smaller stones rattled down into a small, dark hole that appeared, leading back into the hillside.

Caitlin and Connor peered into the darkness. Caitlin wrinkled her nose at the musty smell that flowed out of the darkness.

"It's too small to get through," she said.

"If we move that rock, too," Connor said, "there should be enough room to crawl in."

He hitched the rope to another boulder, and once again his horse pulled steadily and strongly. The second rock came out more easily than the first. A cascade of rocks and dirt rattled down, and Connor coughed as he fanned the dust from the opening with his hat.

"I'll go first," he said.

His large frame barely fit through the opening, but he squeezed into the hole. Caitlin's heart beat fast, and she almost choked on excitement as she knelt to crawl in after him.

What would they find? Was there really a treasure after all?

Connor flicked his lighter, and they stood in the feeble glow, peering into the gloom. It was a small cave, barely the size of a large closet. No strongboxes, no bars of gold lined the walls. The place was empty, except for a small, leather pouch, almost covered with dirt, in one corner.

"Go on, Cait. Pick it up. It's yours," he whispered.

Slowly she knelt and reached for the pouch. It was stiff with age, and the brittle leather cracked as she lifted it from its resting place. Connor held the light closer as she fumbled with the crumbling thong that bound the top of the pouch. She shook the bag, and half a dozen gold coins spilled into her hand.

Connor examined one closely. "Spanish, all right," he said. "Probably from the time of the explorers, around seventeen hundred.'' He dropped the coin back into her cupped palm and it clinked dully against its mates. ''There's your treasure, Cait.''

She shook her head mutely, then crossed the tiny room and crawled out into the dusk, not waiting to see if Connor followed.

Tony had regained consciousness and was struggling against the ropes that held him, cursing loudly. Caitlin stood over him, the coins in her outstretched hand. She was trembling with rage. Her voice shook as she shouted at him.

''There's your treasure, Tony! That's what you killed my parents for. I hope it was worth it!'' She flung the coins in his face and stalked away to bury her face in Ready's mane.

''It can't be! There's more! You're lying to me!'' Tony screamed as he struggled more violently against the ropes. ''There's millions in there. You're just trying to keep it for yourself.'' He twisted his body, trying to worm his way to the cave entrance.

''It's no lie,'' Connor said quietly.

''Yes, it is! It has to be!'' Tony was crying now, tears of rage and frustration.

''I'll show you.'' Connor slipped the blade of Tony's knife against the rope binding his feet and pulled sharply. The rope parted, and Connor dragged Tony to his feet. ''Look for yourself.''

Tony staggered to the cave entrance and pushed his head and shoulders inside. Connor stretched his arm through the hole and flicked the lighter.

''No, no, no!'' Tony's scream was muffled by the rock. He slumped to the floor of the cave, weeping. Connor grabbed his coat collar and dragged him out.

''Where's your horse?'' he asked.

Tony stood sullen and silent, though tears still streamed down his face.

Connor sighed heavily. "I'd just as soon leave you in there and roll the rocks back," he said, "but I'd hate to see your horse suffer if we couldn't find him."

"Over there," Tony muttered and thrust his chin out, indicating a grove of blue spruce. Connor grasped the younger man's coat collar and jerked Tony after him. The pinto mare stood quietly in the shelter of the trees and barely moved as Connor heaved Tony into the saddle. He led the horse back to the spring and tied her to an aspen trunk. Tony sat still, his eyes unfocused, lost in his demented thoughts.

"Are you all right?" Connor touched Caitlin's shoulder. "Can you ride?" She shivered and nodded. He cupped his hands to receive her foot and boosted her up. She swung into the saddle and gathered up the reins.

Connor knelt on the ground where Tony had lain, running his hands through the leaves until he'd found all six coins. "Here." He stood and held them out to Caitlin.

She turned her head away.

Connor shrugged and slipped them into his jeans pocket and mounted up. He led Tony's horse, and Caitlin followed at a little distance.

The fog had lifted a bit, and a few flakes of snow stung their cheeks as a north wind began to moan through the trees. Night was closing in, and soon the horses and riders were only shadowy shapes moving across the pasture. The snow fell thicker and faster.

A light suddenly glowed through the curtain of flakes. Caitlin thought, *The kids must be home from school.*

As they rode into the barnyard, Jeff burst out of the house.

"Cait, where have you been? We were worried."

She tried to dismount, but grimaced and sat still until Connor slipped her arms around her and lifted her to the ground. "Call the sheriff," she said.

Chapter Eighteen

The kitchen was crowded. Tony sat silently while Connor stood close by. Caitlin, her side bandaged and her shirt changed, stood next to Linnie and Jeff at the sink, out of the way of the two sheriff's deputies, while Connor explained what had happened.

"He was really looking for buried treasure?" Deputy Schroeder asked.

"Yes. He had a map and was ready to kill Cait to keep the treasure. But the cave was empty. There was nothing there." Connor's eyes met Caitlin's, warning her to silence.

"Okay." Deputy Schroeder lifted Tony to his feet, and his partner cut the ropes binding his wrists. The click of the handcuffs was loud in the quiet room.

"Take him out to the car, Jim," Schroeder said, "while I get a statement from Miss Morrisey."

Tony moved mechanically, like a sleepwalker. He hadn't spoken since they'd left the hollow. Caitlin wondered if his mind had finally snapped completely.

She sat down at the kitchen table. Jeff and Linnie sat, too, but Connor remained standing, his arms crossed and a scowl on his face.

"Can't this wait until tomorrow?" he said in a growl. "Miss Morrisey's been through a terrible ordeal, and she needs to see a doctor."

Caitlin waved a hand in negation. "It's all right. I'd rather talk now and get it over with. I'm fine."

Deputy Schroeder clicked his pen, opened his notebook to a clean page, and looked inquiringly at Caitlin.

"I can't add much to what Mr. Devlin has already told you," she said. "He—Tony—admitted to me that he engineered our parents' accident, and he planned to kill me, too. By killing me, he hoped to force Linnie and Jeff into selling the ranch to him. Then he would be the legitimate owner of the treasure. He could suddenly 'discover' the gold and become rich."

"But Mr. Devlin said the cave was empty," the deputy said.

Caitlin looked directly into his eyes. "That's right. There was nothing."

"We'll have to go out in the morning and investigate," he answered. "Just to complete the report, you understand. We'll stop by for directions."

Connor interrupted. "Better yet, I'll show you the way. You can drive through the gate in the north pasture."

Deputy Schroeder glanced at Caitlin. "Looks like Mr. Black was the source of your mysterious lights. He probably thought that nighttime would be safer to roam around your property. There would be less chance of being seen."

Caitlin nodded.

"Well, that's all I need," Schroeder said as he clipped his pen back into his shirt pocket. "I'll see you in the morning." He nodded to Connor and left.

They all sat without talking until they heard the engine start and the car pull out of the yard.

Linnie spoke first. "I can't believe it! All the pain he caused us, just for an empty hole in the ground." She buried her head in her arms and sobbed. Caitlin put an arm around her and held her tightly.

"You could have been dead," Jeff said to Caitlin. His eyes misted and he sniffed loudly.

"But I'm not," Caitlin said, "so don't worry."

Linnie spoke up. "All the pain. All for nothing."

Connor dug into his jeans pocket. "Not quite nothing," he said as the gold Spanish coins rolled onto the table.

Linnie and Jeff stared openmouthed at the ancient disks. "You mean there *was* treasure?" Jeff gasped.

"Just those," Caitlin answered. "In a little pouch in the back of the cave."

Jeff picked one up and examined it. "Why didn't you tell the deputy about these?" he asked.

Connor shrugged. "They're not worth much, monetarily. If I'd shown them, they would have been seized for evidence. No telling when you'd get them back. And then, of course, you'd have sightseers and snoops prowling all over your property, hoping to find more 'treasure.' Would you want that?"

"No way," Jeff said.

"So," Connor continued, "I just neglected to mention them to Deputy Schroeder. I'd rather keep them in the family. It'll be something to tell our grandchildren, Cait."

"Grandchildren?" she asked, bewildered.

"Well, after all this, you *are* going to marry me, aren't you?" he said.

"But . . . but . . ." she sputtered.

"Oh, go ahead, Cait. Say yes," Jeff urged. "I'd just as soon have him for a brother-in-law as anyone I know."

"Do, Cait. You know you love him," Linnie said.

"Hold it!" Caitlin shouted. "Can I at least have until morning to think about it?"

"Well, of course," Connor said, "but I'll be back early for your answer." He leaned over and kissed her soundly, then shrugged into his torn coat.

"Be careful of your arm," Caitlin warned.

"It'll be fine by morning," he said. "And when I come back, we'll go into town and have a doctor look at you.

"Jeff, I don't want to get my horse out again in this storm. Can I leave him here overnight?"

"Sure. I'll drive you home. It's not that far," Jeff said in answer to Caitlin's protest. "I'll be back in a few minutes."

"Oh, all right," she conceded. "But be careful. You aren't street legal yet."

Connor and Jeff left, and Linnie brought her sister a cup of herbal tea. Caitlin sipped it slowly, allowing her mind and body to relax finally. By the time Jeff returned, she was sound asleep, slumped over the kitchen table.

"Yes, you can stay home from school," Caitlin said the next morning.

"Oh, boy! Can I go with Connor when the sheriff comes out?" Jeff asked.

"I doubt they'll let you," she said. "It's an official investigation, after all."

She laughed at his crestfallen look. "But when they get back, you can ride Rough out and take a look for yourself. Look. The snow's melting already."

The sun shone brightly in the blue October sky, and a few fluffy clouds ringed the horizon.

"Can I go, too?" Linnie spoke from the hall doorway.

"Sure," Caitlin said. "I'll feel better with both of you going, but be sure to take a flashlight."

Jeff finished his scrambled eggs and glass of milk. "I can't believe I took people there all summer to picnic and never suspected a thing," he said. "When they find out what they missed, will they be mad!"

"And just how will they find out?" Caitlin asked.

"I'll tell 'em next summer. We'll go for another trail ride and I'll tell 'em all the story of how Tony did us wrong and how Connor caught him and how you crawled into the cave with only a cigarette lighter—"

"Hold it," Caitlin said. "You're assuming some of our guests will come back next year."

"Well, sure," he said. "Who wouldn't want to come back here?"

She smiled at his enthusiasm. "Let's hope you're right."

"Of course I am. Hey, here's Connor."

Connor knocked briefly and opened the door. "Good morning. How are you?" He gathered Caitlin into his arms and kissed her thoroughly.

"Fine," she replied when she'd caught her breath.

"Excuse me," Jeff said. "I just remembered something I have to take care of upstairs." He jumped up from the table and jerked his head at Linnie.

"Oh, I think I left my curling iron plugged in," she said, and followed Jeff out of the room.

"Subtlety isn't their strong point," Connor said, smiling down at Caitlin. "I think they want us to be alone."

Caitlin smiled back. "I wonder why?"

"Maybe they think you have something to tell me," he said softly.

"Maybe I do," she whispered.

His lips sought hers once again, and her body melted into his as they clung together in a timeless kiss.

At last their lips parted. His sky blue eyes questioned her.

One word fell from her lips. "Yes."

"Oh, Cait." He held her close and stroked her hair. "I love you, Cait."

She drew away and pointed to the gold coins still scattered on the table. "Are you sure you aren't after me for my money?" she asked with a twinkle in her eye.

He glanced at the Spanish coins and shook his head. "You're the only treasure I'll ever need."

As he kissed her again, she knew it was true.